COUNT DRACULA, ME AND NORMA D.

JESSICA HATCHIGAN lives in Detroit with her husband and two children and works as a reporter for the *Detroit Legal News*.

COUNT DRACULA, ME AND NORMA D.

JESSICA HATCHIGAN

AN AVON  CAMELOT BOOK

COUNT DRACULA, ME AND NORMA D. is an original publication of Avon Books. This work has never before appeared in book form.

AVON BOOKS
A division of
The Hearst Corporation
105 Madison Avenue
New York, New York 10016

Library of Congress in Publication Data:
Hatchigan, Jessica.
    Count Dracula, me and Norma D.

    (An Avon Camelot book)
    Summary: When she's not trying to convince her friends that she has extrasensory powers, ten-year-old Mollie finds ways to promote her mother's Chocky Chunka cookie business.
    [1. Extrasensory perception—Fiction. 2. Friendship—Fiction] I. Title.
PZ7.H2818Co   1987   [Fic]   87-18737

First Camelot Printing: November 1987

CAMELOT TRADEMARK REG. U.S. PAT. OFF. AND IN OTHER COUNTRIES, MARCA REGISTRADA, HECHO EN U.S.A.

Printed in the U.S.A.

OPM   10 9 8 7 6 5 4 3 2

To my children, Jenny and Jim

COUNT DRACULA, ME AND NORMA D.

Chapter One
The After-School Séance

"Do you think he'll catch us?"

That was Lori Walker talking. In the flickering candlelight I could see her glasses flash like a couple of jack-o'-lanterns as she turned her head toward the door. Lori was skinny and nervous and smart. She was only nine but she was a fifth-grader, like the rest of us. That was because she was so smart she'd been double-promoted in kindergarten.

"Shhh," I said, squinting my eyes shut. "You're wrecking my concentration."

This was my first séance. I'd told Lori and Norma and Clare and Janet that I had ESP and that I could get the spirits to tell their fortunes, but the truth was I didn't really know if there were any spirits in the Digbert Brothers Funeral Home, or if I had ESP, or—once we were sitting around the candle and waiting for things to happen—why I'd come up with this idea at all.

1

"Molly Harter, if you don't hurry it up, I'm going to wreck *you*. You're going to get all of us in trouble."

That was Norma, of course. Being her normal self. Even during a séance she had to boss everyone around. Norma lived in the funeral home, in the upstairs part of the building. But she was probably the only person in the room who didn't know that the rest of us thought the place was haunted. That was because, probably, nobody dared to tell her.

"Norma," I said, opening my eyes a little, "you said your uncle wouldn't find us in the embalming room."

"The embalming room!" Lori said. She started to shake. "I—I didn't know this was the *embalming* room."

Norma ignored Lori.

"Look, Molly, I said Uncle John *probably* wouldn't find us in here *if* we only stayed for a few *minutes,* but we've been here for almost a *half hour* and you still haven't told everyone's fortune. If Uncle John *does* find us in here, I'm going to be in *big* trouble with Mom and Dad when they get back from their cruise. Besides, this séance is getting *boring*. So hurry it up, all right?"

I sighed and squinted my eyes shut again. When I opened them I stared into the glass ball I held on my lap. But I couldn't concentrate.

For the first time I started to wonder if holding a Halloween séance in the Digbert Brothers Funeral Home was really such a great idea after all. Nothing was happening the way I thought it would.

Or was it? Goose bumps started to speckle my arms. I rubbed my hands up and down them, but it didn't make the goose bumps go away. It was only late afternoon, about three o'clock, but in the darkness of the embalming room it could have been midnight.

"It—it's r-r-really c-c-creepy in here," Lori stuttered.

Lori was right. It *was* creepy. *Really* creepy. I tried to

2

breathe deeply. Mom says that's what I should do when I'm getting nervous. But as I was breathing I looked up. The silver gurney that stood against the back wall of the room caught my eye and the smell of formaldehyde in the air choked me. I had to wrap my arms around my stomach tightly to stop myself from heaving.

"*Molly*," someone whispered.

I looked up. It was Janet Anders. She was new at Ferlinghetti Elementary this year. She was tall and skinny and she had long brown hair that she wore in pigtails on either side of her head. She reminded me of the picture of Pocahontas in our social studies book.

"Are you okay?" she asked. "You seem kind of down."

"I'm all right," I said. "I'm fine."

I was a little touchy when I said it. Janet and I weren't really friends yet. Anyway, not friends enough for me to talk to her about anything private.

"Who cares if she's up, or if she's down, or if she's sideways?" Norma Digbert said. "Let's hurry up and get this over with."

Norma was looking at her watch and tapping her fingers on her knee.

"You're sure h-he's not going to catch us?" Lori asked again, looking back over her shoulder at the door.

"Oh, be quiet, Lori," Norma hissed impatiently, "or she'll never get this over with."

"Maybe Lori's right to be worried," Clare said, "we probably shouldn't be here at all. We might get in trouble."

I hated hearing Clare talking like that. Until a couple of weeks ago, when she and Norma had made the junior varsity cheerleading squad together, Clare had been my best friend.

"If you're so worried about getting caught, Clare, you

3

shouldn't have come," I said. "Anyway, you were the one who told me this place was haunted and would make a great place for a séance."

Norma looked at Clare, her lips pressed together tightly.

"Did you say that, Clare? Did you say that the funeral home was haunted?"

Clare glared at me.

"You really have a big mouth, Molly."

She turned to Norma.

"Look, Norma, *everyone* says this place is haunted."

"Clare, *I* happen to live here."

"Uh, maybe it's just the main floor that's haunted," Clare said.

Even in the dim light I could see the angry V form between Norma's eyebrows.

Clare tried to change the subject. "Okay, Molly, you told Lori her future. How she's going to be a college professor and marry a rock star and write a best-seller about karate. But what about me? What's going to happen to me?"

For the second time that afternoon I picked up my blue Scripto pencil and started to scribble on one of my index cards. After a couple of minutes I stopped writing, laid the pencil down, and folded the card in half. I handed it to Clare. Clare grabbed it and started to open it. But I stopped her.

"Not yet," I said, holding out my hand.

Clare looked miffed, but she reached into her back jeans pocket and dug out two quarters. She handed them over to me. Then she read through her card.

"Five kids!" she yelled all of a sudden.

Everyone jumped.

"I write it the way the spirits send the impressions to me," I said.

4

"Then the spirits are crazy," Clare said. "I'm going to New York and become a famous fashion model. I want my fifty cents back."

"Sorry," I said, dropping the coins into the blue velvet gin bag Dad had let me have last Christmas when he visited us from Ohio. "This money is for the class trip to the science museum, and I'm not giving any refunds. Plus, I'd appreciate your keeping it down. I still have two fortunes to go."

"I don't know why you couldn't just earn your field trip money by doing chores for your mom, the way Mrs. Marnock told us to," Clare said.

I frowned and looked down at my hands. If she were still my best friend, Clare would know how tough things were at home, moneywise, since the divorce.

"Molly," Janet said, "I didn't get my fortune done yet."

"Why bother?" Clare piped up. "You'll probably find out you're going to end up as the Fat Lady at the circus."

Janet ignored Clare. I would have too, if I was her. Janet was probably the skinniest girl in the fifth grade.

"But hurry it up. Okay, Molly?" Janet said. "I don't think I can stand staying in here another ten minutes."

"Oh?" Norma Digbert said. Her voice was cold. "And just what's *wrong* with this place?"

"Look," Janet said, "I know you live here. But that's upstairs—*not* in the embalming room."

"Those stories about the funeral home being haunted are all made up," Norma said. When she finished talking, the V between her eyebrows was the darkest and deepest I'd ever seen it. Norma was really proud of living in the funeral home. She thought it was cool. She bragged about it the way other kids brag about getting mopeds for Christmas.

Norma Digbert had never been one of my favorite

people. And I knew I wasn't one of hers. I also knew she'd only agreed to let me hold the séance in her funeral home because of the dollar I was going to give her. The Digbert family had a reputation for being greedy. Norma was no exception.

My Scripto started to move over an index card again.

This time I handed the paper to Janet. Janet opened it and took a look. She started giggling. "'First woman on the moon'" she said. "Molly, you're nuts! I'm afraid of heights. Uh, by the way, astronaut is spelled N-A-U-T, not N-O-T."

"I guess the spirits need to hit the old spelling book," Norma said, and sniggered.

Finally it was Norma's turn. I passed my hands over the crystal ball and stared deeply into it.

"Ah," I said, "the crystal ball once again speaks to me."

"Oh, come on," Clare said. "That's not a crystal ball. It's just an old paperweight. My mom has one just like it."

My eyes flicked up. I stared at Clare. Hard.

"Clare Blain," I said, "how dare you mock the crystal ball that has been handed down in my family from the time of the ancient Egyptians?"

"Will you guys keep it *down?*" Norma hissed. "If my Uncle John finds out we're in here, I'll be in big trouble. This place is supposed to be off-limits."

For a minute I wondered what kind of punishment Norma got when she was in trouble. Scrubbing gurneys? Polishing caskets? I shuddered.

"Besides," Norma said, glancing at her wrist watch, "it's three forty-five. You said we'd be out of here by half past."

My hand raced over the paper. When I finished writing I handed the card over to Norma.

6

She opened it and scowled. Her voice was sarcastic.

"Thanks a lot, Molly," she said. "I really appreciate it, but for your information, they don't put kids in chain gangs."

"Things can change," I said.

"Uh, let's blow out the candle," Clare said, "and get out of here."

Just then something funny happened—something really funny. It was like this little explosion went off in my head—a flash, like a light bulb popping off. A second later there was a picture in my head. The picture I saw was of a tall man in a dark suit, a man with a long white face.

I couldn't see the face too clearly. I couldn't tell if the man was a ghost or a real person. But I knew, even without seeing his face, that there was something creepy about him, and when his picture appeared in my mind I had this peculiar feeling that something terrible was about to happen, and the tall man in the dark suit was going to make it happen.

The next thing that happened, just after my flash, was even weirder: Just as Clare was taking in a big breath to blow out the candle there was a sudden whoosh and *it went out on its own*.

Everyone screamed, jumped up, and rushed for the door. But when we got to it something was blocking the way out! Something cold and hard.

"The gurney!" Lori yelled.

"But it was on the other side of the room!" Clare screamed.

Before anyone could move the gurney we heard a horrible sound. *Heavy footsteps*. Heavy footsteps that were getting louder. That were coming in our direction. With an awful screech the door to the embalming room suddenly flew open and in the light from the outside corri-

7

dor I could see him! It was the man I'd seen in the picture in my mind. The man with the long white face.

He was standing there, blocking our way.

It wasn't a ghost; it was worse: It was Mr. Digbert.

Chapter Two
I Get the Blues

"Well, this is terrific," Norma said when the five of us finally were allowed to leave the funeral home.

The warm October sun felt good after the embalming room and what seemed like a two-thousand-year-long lecture.

"A whole week," Norma was saying. "I'm grounded for a whole week. You guys were really dumb."

"Dumb?" Clare said angrily. "You were there. You heard that whooshing sound."

I was a little surprised that Clare was actually angry at Norma. I shouldn't have been too surprised though. Clare had always been very touchy. She'd never been a terrific best friend.

"Clare," Norma said, "that whooshing sound was the ventilation system switching on, that's all."

"Well, what about the gurney?" Lori asked. "Don't tell us the ventilation system whooshed *that* from the back of the room to the door."

"Of course it didn't," Norma said. "One of you must have snagged your jacket onto it or something and pulled it over when we all ran for the door."

"Uh, Norma," Lori said. "Nobody's wearing a jacket."

"I said, 'or something,'" Norma snapped. "Anyway," she added, turning toward me with a glare, "I wouldn't be surprised if Molly set that whole thing up."

I glared back at her.

"Uh, I've got to go," Janet said quickly, pulling at the sleeve of my T-shirt. "Want to come along, Molly?"

Janet and I started walking away.

"Don't bother to say good-bye," Norma yelled after us sarcastically.

We just kept on walking.

Janet stopped when we reached Sandhill Street.

"This is where I turn," she said.

She walked a few steps down Sandhill Street, then turned to wave good-bye. I waved back.

When I reached home I stepped into the house, took a deep breath, and tried to relax. The house, as usual, smelled like chocolate-chip cookies. That's because Mom runs her chocolate-chip cookie business from our house. Our basement is a chocolate-chip cookie factory. My mom's name is Hattie Harter. The cookies she makes are called Hattie Harter Chocky Chunkas.

I threw my books onto the hall table and walked into the rec room. My sister Nikki was lying on the floor looking at a *Vogue*. Nikki is my older sister. She's thirteen. She's pretty and has a lot of friends and gets straight A's in school. Without even trying.

"Hi, Nikki," I said.

Nikki nodded. She didn't look up from her magazine.

"Where's Becka?" I asked.

Becka is my little sister. She's four.

"Outside," Nikki said, wrinkling her forehead. I could tell she wanted me to leave her and her magazine alone. When she was reading she didn't go in for long answers.

"Nikki," I asked, "do you know Mr. Digbert?"

"Which one? There are two Mr. D's, aren't there?"

"This one is Norma Digbert's uncle. He lives in the funeral home with Norma and her family."

"Uh-huh. I know him."

I told Nikki what had happened. She put down her magazine and listened.

When I finished she let out a low whistle.

"Boy, Molly," she said. "A séance? You sure do some weird things."

I ignored that.

"Do you think he'll call Mom?" I asked.

"What do you think?" Nikki was twirling a strand of long blond hair that she'd wrapped around her finger. I thought about Mr. Digbert—about his long white face and his thin tight lips. And then I thought about the awful feeling I'd had in the funeral home just before he walked into the embalming room.

"He'll call," I said.

I'd had a feeling like that once before. It had happened just a few days before Halloween—that was what had given me the idea for the séance. I had been sitting in the rec room reading an old Nancy Drew of Nikki's when all of a sudden this picture flashed in my mind. It was a picture of Grandma Mundy. She was punching the buttons on the wall phone in her apartment. Ten seconds later the rec room phone started ringing. I answered it. It was Grandma Mundy!

Thinking about my first flash and then thinking about the awful feeling I'd had in the funeral home about Mr. Digbert made goose bumps break out on my arms. But there wasn't anything I could do about it, so I tried really hard to put it out of my mind.

We ate dinner early, around five, because Mom was going to take Becka trick-or-treating as soon as it got dark, and Nikki was going to a party. Becka and Nikki wore their Halloween costumes at dinner. Becka was a fuzzy pink bunny with big floppy ears and Nikki was a princess—with a crown, jewels, and everything.

The costumes were great. Really neat. Grandma Mundy had made them. Grandma Mundy used to be a dressmaker. She retired six years ago. Until then she'd had a store on Parker Avenue with a sign in the window that read

ELLEN MUNDY'S
CLOTHING MADE TO ORDER

Mom came into the dining room carrying a platter of hamburgers. She blinked when she saw me.

"Molly," she said, "I know you don't want to go trick-or-treating this year, but aren't you going to dress in a costume to give out treats?"

"I told Grandma not to make me a costume this year, Mom."

Mom looked at me a few seconds more, as if she was wondering what was going on.

"I'm too old to go trick-or-treating," I said, "and I didn't get invited to any parties."

"But, Molly, you always loved dressing for Halloween."

I didn't say anything, just shrugged my shoulders, and started to squirt ketchup on a hamburger.

"Well, sweetheart, if you change your mind there are some old Halloween costumes of Nikki's in one of the basement closets."

I think Mom was going to say something else, but Nikki butted in with how she'd just placed second in the big fall swim meet at Ferlinghetti High. Mom started listening. I guess she forgot all about the fact that I wasn't wearing a costume to give out treats on Halloween, because she didn't say any more about it after that.

It got dark pretty fast. Mom and Becka left. Nikki went down the street to her party. I put the basket of Chocky Chunka sample packs on the table in the foyer and then waited for witches and gorillas and space monsters and ghouls to ring our doorbell.

After a few minutes of passing out treats I began to wonder if maybe I'd been wrong to tell Grandma to forget about sewing me a costume this year. I mean, all the trick-or-treaters I saw were having a great time. And then I remembered how much fun it had been last year, pretending to be somebody else. Besides, I thought, if I were dressed up in a costume and pretending to be a cowgirl or a ghost it would help me to forget about Mr. Digbert and his promise that he'd call Mom.

I remembered what Mom had said—about the costumes in the basement closet. I gave treats to the latest bunch of trick-or-treaters, then I closed the front door and went down to the basement.

There was a great costume in the closet. It was Nikki's witch hat and dress from a couple of Halloweens ago. I put it on. It fit me perfectly. I rummaged around the basement for a while, looking for Halloween makeup. But I couldn't find any.

Then I got a terrific idea. I ran upstairs to the kitchen and found a bottle of blue food coloring. It was the kind Mom used to tint cake icing. The doorbell was ringing, but I had enough time to fly into the bathroom and splash the coloring all over my face and hands. It looked great. Really blue.

Next I grabbed Mom's broom from the kitchen closet and ran to pull open the door for the next batch of trick-or-treaters, yelling, "Nyah, hah, hah," in this high screechy voice and waving my broom around.

Most of the kids just looked at me with bored expressions and held out their bags for the cookies. But I scared one little kid. Sammy Conklin, our next-door neighbor. His mother got mad at me, and when I told her Halloween was supposed to be about *tricks* as well as *treats* she just wrinkled her nose at me, grabbed the pack of cookies I was holding out for Sammy, and turned and walked away.

It wasn't my fault Sammy was such a scaredy-cat.

The phone rang. Three times. Once it was Grandma Mundy. Another time it was a lady from the PTA. And then it was a college student who was selling magazines.

Each time I heard the rings start up I just about jumped out of my blue skin. But by around nine o'clock —when the trick-or-treating was beginning to wind down—I began to relax a little. Mr. Digbert hadn't called. Maybe my flash had been all wrong and I'd been worried about nothing.

I took in a deep breath and let out a big sigh of relief.

A minute later Mom and Becka stepped through the front door. A second later the phone rang. My mouth felt dry and my heart was pounding as I answered it. An awful low voice answered back. It was Mr. Digbert. He wanted to talk to Mom.

Mom was just kicking off her shoes and slumping onto the couch in the living room. She got up to take the call.

After Mom hung up the phone I found something out: When you're little and you get a spanking for doing something wrong, it hurts pretty bad. But when you're ten years old the look in your Mom's eyes that says you

14

let her down can hurt even worse than a spanking. That was the look my mom had in her eyes that Halloween night.

"I'm sorry, Mom," I said in a low voice.

Mom said, "All right, dear. Let's just make sure I don't have to hear about anything like this again."

I felt bad. But I felt a little angry too. Mom acted as if I planned to hold séances in Mr. Digbert's embalming room the same way I went to McDonald's for a Big Mac and a Coke.

Mom was about to go sit down again when she stopped herself and took a closer look at my face.

"Molly Harter," Mom said, "what kind of makeup *is* that on your face?"

"Food coloring," I said.

"Food coloring?" Mom said.

"What's wrong?" I asked. "What's the matter?"

Mom sighed.

"Molly, dear, don't you know that food coloring doesn't wash off?"

"Huh?"

It was a good thing I was wearing the witch hat, because I could feel my hair popping up underneath it.

"It doesn't wash off? You mean I'll be like this *forever?*"

I looked in the dining room mirror. My blue face looked back at me.

"Not *forever,* Molly. But it will take at least a few days to wear off. Maybe even a week or so."

"What!"

I wasn't too thrilled. I thought about going to school with a blue face. I thought about Norma and Clare, about the two of them seeing me with my face as blue as a Crayola crayon.

Nikki got back from her party. She blinked when she

15

saw me. Mom told her what had happened. Nikki stared at me some more, her mouth sort of twisty. I could tell exactly what she was thinking. She was embarrassed at the idea of having a sister with a blue face.

I ran into the bathroom. I scrubbed and scrubbed and scrubbed. But Mom was right. The coloring didn't come off.

Even my little sister stared at me when I stepped out of the bathroom.

"Molly," she said, "you're blue."

I wanted to scream. I was pretty sure that I was living the most awful day of my whole life.

Bedtime finally rolled around. But I couldn't sleep.

I sat up and then thumped my head back down hard on my pillow. That didn't help. I tried counting sheep. That didn't help.

I got up out of bed and walked over to the window. I sat down in the big green easy chair Mom had let me have when she'd redecorated the living room a few years ago. I looked outside and I thought about how terrible it was going to be showing up for school tomorrow with blue food coloring all over my face.

I guess I must have fallen asleep there, because when my eyes finally flicked open, the morning sun was out and it was shining like a spotlight all over my bright blue hands.

Chapter Three
A Friend with a Calendar

"Hey, get a load of Bluebeard," Eddie Kleeg said.

Eddie was the fattest kid in the fifth grade, and maybe the meanest too.

"What happened, Molly?" Kevin Sanders asked. "Chow down on too many blueberries?"

Kevin thought he was a great comedian.

"Uh-unh," Norma said. "She just forgot to put on her makeup."

That's how it was. Everybody made jokes. I couldn't exactly blame them. I guess it wasn't every day you saw a fifth-grader with a blue face and hands sitting in your classroom.

Naturally Norma got in the most digs. At recess when we were all on the playground she pointed at me and whispered something to Clare and Carrie Miner and Jackie Kendall. The four of them looked at me and giggled.

I turned my back to them. I tried not to remember that Jackie and Carrie had been my friends.

"Ignore those dopes."

I looked up. It was Janet Anders. Lori was with her.

"Janet's right," Lori said. "Just ignore them. You, uh, don't look that bad."

"Oh, sure," I said.

Lori laughed.

It was funny. Lori was the nervous, shaky type. But here she was, being my friend while I was walking around with a freaky blue face. She didn't care what Norma and the other kids thought.

"Did Mr. Digbert call your mom?" Janet asked.

I nodded. I told Janet and Lori about Mr. Digbert's call.

"I hate him," I said. "I hate him more than I hate anybody else in the world."

Just then Norma ran by. She was playing tag with Clare and Jackie and Carrie.

"Watch out!" Lori yelled.

Before I had a chance to realize what was happening Norma bumped against me. Hard. I probably would have fallen over backward except that Janet grabbed my arm and broke my fall. Janet was angry.

"Norma Digbert, you did that on purpose!" Janet yelled.

Norma stopped running for a second, turned around, looked straight at me, and yelled, *"Weirdo!"* loud enough for everyone on the playground to hear. Then she ran off again.

Clare and Jackie and Carrie ran after her. They didn't stop to see if I was okay. They didn't care that Norma had almost knocked me down. Or that she'd insulted me.

"Creeps," Janet said.

18

"If she calls me a name one more time . . ." I said. My voice was shaking. I was glad when the end-of-recess bell rang.

The afternoon was pretty quiet, but I couldn't stop thinking about what had happened at recess. It was sort of depressing.

When the school bell finally rang, I took my time about packing my backpack. I made sure I waited until everybody left before I finally closed the flaps and started trudging out of the classroom. I knew I'd have to walk home alone. Who'd want to walk home with somebody who had a blue face?

But when I finally left the classroom and stepped out into the corridor, Janet was standing there. She was leaning against one of the lockers, with her backpack dangling from her hands. "I thought I'd wait for you," she said.

The two of us left the building together and started up Morningside Street. The next day after school we walked home together again. We walked home together for the rest of the week. Janet was an okay person to talk to. I found out that she liked books about dogs and horses, just like me. And that her favorite rock group was the Tunetasticks, the same as mine. And that she loved Moon Pies, my favorite dessert next to Chocky Chunkas.

The next week, on Monday, when we got to Sandhill Street, instead of walking away and waving good-bye, Janet asked if we could do our homework together.

"Okay," I said. "The only thing is we have to do it at my house. Mom asked me to watch my little sister for her today. Our regular baby-sitter has the flu and my sister Nikki's at swim team practice."

Janet said studying at my house was okay with her. Then she asked me where Mom was going.

19

"Out selling cookies."

"Selling cookies? Is she with the Girl Scouts or something?"

I explained about Mom's chocolate-chip cookie business.

We kept talking. We talked all the way from school to my house.

Janet asked me about my ESP.

"Do you really have it, Molly? Or were you just kidding?"

"I—I don't know," I said. "I'm not sure. All I know is a couple of times I've gotten these flashes—where I've known something was going to happen and then it did."

"Wow," Janet said.

We were just passing by the big bushes that separate the Conklins' yard from ours when all of a sudden we froze in our tracks. A horrible growling sound was filling the air. It seemed to come out of nowhere.

"What's *that?*" Janet asked.

"I don't know."

Just then, out of the corner of my eye, I saw a green blur whiz out of the bushes behind us. It rammed my knees. My books shot out of my hands, all over the pavement, and I almost fell on top of them. I gasped and turned around.

The green blur was Becka.

"Aargh!" she snorted. "Grrr-rr-rr!"

She was circling us like a rocket in orbit—faster and faster and faster. All the time she kept growling and snuffling.

Janet looked startled.

"Hey, what's going on?" she asked.

Becka ran in front of us, flopped over, and started rolling around on the pavement. She was still snorting and growling. Loudly.

"Oh," I said, bending over to pick up my scattered books, "she's pretending to be a dinosaur. Becka loves animals, and that's her favorite one right now. It used to be penguins, but last month Grandma Mundy took her to the natural science museum and they had dinosaur bones there."

Janet laughed. Becka stopped rolling around for a minute and smiled up at her.

"What's that book you're holding?" Janet asked her.

Becka held it up. On the cover was a picture of a huge green monster with a long tail and a tiny head. The title was *Big Blimpy, A Day in the Life of a Dinosaur*.

"*My* book," Becka said.

"Grandma bought it for her," I told Janet. "She's made Nikki and me read it to her about two zillion times."

Two seconds later Becka was up on her feet.

"Read it," she said to Janet. "Read *Big Blimpy*."

"Becka," I said, "we've got homework to do. Why don't you go play with Sammy Conklin?"

"He ran away," Becka said. "A dinosaur bit him."

"Oh, Becka! Hard?"

She nodded, smiling. Janet burst out laughing.

We walked into the house. Janet plopped down on the rec room sofa with Becka, opened the dinosaur book, and began to read.

She was a pretty good reader. She made the boring dinosaur story sound exciting.

While I was tossing my books down onto the coffee table in the rec room, I could hear Mom in the kitchen. She was on the phone.

A few seconds later I heard Mom calling me.

As I walked into the kitchen, Mom hung up the phone and began packing bags of Chocky Chunkas into a large cardboard carton she'd placed on the kitchen counter.

21

"Molly," she said, smiling up at me, "I've got an errand for you to run."

I noticed that Mom was dressed in her best suit, a pretty yellow one. I could tell she was in a hurry.

"Aggie Plimpton from the Food-a-Rama called. She wants fifty bags of cookies right away. Since I'm running late for my sales appointment, and the Food-a-Rama is three blocks out of my way, I thought maybe you could take these cookies over to her in your wagon."

"Sure, Mom. Can Janet come with me?"

"Janet?" Mom said.

"She's—a new friend. From school."

"I don't see why not," Mom said. "You'll have to take Becka along too, of course. And remember, you have to be there before four. The Food-a-Rama closes early on Mondays."

"Mom," I said as I suddenly noticed the new calendar that was hanging on the kitchen wall next to the phone. "What's that?"

Mom looked up at the calendar.

"It's just a calendar, dear."

"I know that, Mom, but what I mean is, well, it says 'Digbert Brothers Funeral Home.' Nobody we know died, did they?"

Mom smiled.

"No, Molly. Nobody died. Mr. Digbert brought it over as a gift when he stopped by today."

"Mr. Digbert was here today?"

"Well, yes. It seems the custodian at the funeral parlor was cleaning up this morning and he found a paperweight of yours. Just after you left for school Mr. Digbert called and told me he could stop by and drop it off. He brought the calendar along. We got to talking. He was so charming that I asked him to stay for coffee. That's all."

22

Mom had hardly finished her last sentence before she was rushing for the door. A second later it clicked closed behind her. The house seemed extra quiet all of a sudden. I heard Mom's car start up and rumble out of the driveway. I went over to the Digbert Brothers Funeral Home calendar and stared at it. I could feel the little hairs on the back of my neck pricking up.

Mr. Digbert having coffee with Mom? Mr. Digbert *charming?*

Chapter Four
The Cookies Crumble

A few seconds later I calmed down. I decided I wasn't going to let my imagination run wild on me. I wasn't going to let myself think about all sorts of terrible things that were never going to happen, that just *couldn't* happen.

I went back to the rec room. Janet was finishing the last few pages of Becka's book. It really was a dumb story.

> ...*and then*, [she read] *Big Blimpy walked back home.*
> *SNAP! CRUNCH! POP!*
> *The twigs broke under his feet.*
> *Big Blimpy found his nest! He climbed in!*
> *SNAP! CRUNCH! POP! went the twigs and the grass.*
> *"AHHHH!" Big Blimpy said.*
> *He went to sleep.*
> *SNORE, SNORE, SNORE.*

Big Blimpy was snug. And he was safe. And he was happy. He was the happiest dinosaur in the ancient forest.

"Janet," I said, "Mom wants us to run an errand for her."

Janet got up. Becka popped up next to her.

"Me too?" she said.

"Uh-huh," I said. "Mom said you should come along."

Becka followed us into the kitchen, where we grabbed hold of the carton of cookies, and out the back door to the garage where my wagon was.

"Be careful," I told Janet as we put the carton into the wagon. "We don't want any cookies to break. Mom's motto is 'Hattie Harter stands for quality.' She says that means we have to make sure all our cookies are in one piece when we sell them."

I picked up the wagon handle and started to pull it down the driveway. Janet walked beside me. Becka trailed behind the wagon.

"Where's your mom going today?" Janet asked when we reached the end of Morningside Street and crossed over to Forrester.

"She's got an appointment with Fred Glemp. He owns the Farmer Fred food store chain. Farmer Fred's is the biggest supermarket chain in Michigan. Mom says if she could convince Mr. Glemp to buy her cookies for his Farmer Fred stores, then the bank would give her a loan so that she could buy some more equipment for her cookie factory and hire some people to work for her."

"Wow," Janet said. She gave a low whistle. "It must be pretty exciting, having a mother in the cookie business."

"I don't know," I said, shrugging. I thought about

25

Mom sitting at her desk and staring at all the bills she had to pay, and about how she had told me that Mr. Glemp was a hard person to sell anything to.

"Molly, I'm tired."

That was Becka. She did look kind of tired. I guess three blocks is a long walk for a four-year-old.

"Can I ride?" Becka asked.

"No, Becka. You can't ride. There's no room on the wagon."

"Please," Becka said.

I looked at my Star Wars watch. If we didn't get to the Food-a-Rama in ten minutes, it would be closed.

"Ple-e-e-ease," Becka said again. This time she'd stopped walking and her hands were on her hips. Knowing Becka I was pretty sure that if we didn't give her a ride she would stand exactly where she was until just about the end of the world.

I groaned. "Oh, *okay,*" I said. I bent over and shoved the carton of cookies as far back in the wagon as it would go. There was a tiny space left. Becka clambered into the wagon. When she scrunched herself up a little she just fit.

We hurried on. Soon we reached Parker Avenue.

I liked Parker Avenue. To me it seemed like the busiest street in the world. It was always noisy and exciting. Trucks and cars stopped for the light where Forrester Street crossed the avenue and then whizzed on. Besides that, you could see great stuff on Parker Avenue.

The police emergency phone, for instance. It hung on a pole next to the cross light. It had a blue light over it. Nikki said that the emergency phone was where you ran to make a call if anyone was about to mug you.

And then there was the Parker Avenue sewer. There was always something wrong with the Parker Avenue sewer. Ever since I could remember, every few months

26

workmen would come around and open up another stretch of the sewer. This time they'd opened the sewer just in front of the sausage shop. There was a rail around the hole but you could see the ladder going down into it. The openings that led into the sewer always looked deep and mysterious to me — like caves.

And then, of course, there were the stores. Besides Farmer Fred's there were a lot of other stores on Parker Avenue, including the Food-a-Rama. I looked down the street from the sausage shop and ten yards away I could see the big sign painted on the side of Mrs. Plimpton's store. It said:

FOOD-A-RAMA
GOURMET TREATS!
LOTS OF EATS!

There was a picture on the sign of Mrs. Plimpton holding a tray of éclairs. Mrs. Plimpton looked as big as a house. The green dress she was wearing looked like a tent, and her head looked like a little round knob on top of a big round mountain. It was a pretty good picture. It looked just like her.

I looked at my watch. It was five to four. We had made it in time after all.

That was when I heard it. The horrible sound.

"*What* was that?" Janet asked.

We both turned around at the same time.

"Becka!" I shouted.

Becka was sinking into the carton of Chocky Chunkas.

"SNAP!" Becka shouted. She had a big smile on her face. "SNAP! CRUNCH! POP!"

She was lucky her bottom was hidden in the bags of

Chocky Chunkas because I think that if it wasn't I would have smacked it.

"SNAP! CRUNCH! POP!" Becka yelled again.

Then she looked at my face and she stopped smiling. I was too mad to even yell at her.

Janet helped me to lift her out. I bent down and looked into the carton and groaned.

"I can't deliver these cookies to Mrs. Plimpton," I said. "They're all smashed."

Janet looked worried.

"All of them?" she asked. She reached in for a bag and pulled it out. It looked flat as a pancake, and the paper was all wrinkled.

Janet didn't want to give up. She shook the bag and some of the wrinkles plumped out. She did it to some more of the bags of smashed cookies.

"It's no use," I said. "Even if the bags look okay, the cookies are still broken."

"Are you sure?"

I picked up one of the bags Janet had plumped up and shook it. It sounded like sand sloshing around in a pail.

"I—I can't deliver these. Mom's really strict about never selling broken cookies. We give them to the poor."

I turned around to where Becka had been standing. I was about to tell her that I wished we could give *her* to the poor too. But Becka wasn't there.

"Oh, no!" I yelled. "Where is she?"

Janet and I looked up and down the street. Cars whooshed by. A boy on a bicycle zipped past us. But we couldn't see Becka anywhere.

She was gone.

I swallowed hard. It felt like a big heavy billiard ball was going down my throat. I looked down Parker Avenue.

Janet didn't say anything but her eyes were shiny at the corners.

"C'mon, Janet," I said. "Let's walk around and look for her. Maybe she's just hiding."

We left the wagon where it was and began to look around.

There was no place for Becka to hide. There weren't any bushes big enough for her to crawl behind and the buildings didn't have any nooks or crannies for her to slip into. We looked everywhere. We even ran three stores down to the Toy Shopperie, Becka's favorite store. The clerk said she hadn't seen Becka.

When we got out of the toy store I knew what I had to do. Janet and I walked to the police emergency phone next to the cross light. I picked up the phone and after a few seconds I heard a man's voice. The man on the phone asked me a lot of questions—my name, where I was, how old Becka was, and how long ago she'd disappeared.

I was just about to answer his last question when a hand closed over mine. A big fat hand.

"Now that's enough of that," a voice from behind me said, and the hand pulled the phone away and hung it back on its hook.

I looked up. A fat lady in a green dress was standing behind me. It was Mrs. Plimpton. She looked annoyed.

"Don't you know, young lady, that that is a police phone, and not a toy? Now you stop playing and bring those cookies in. It's past my closing time, you know."

"But—but—"

"Now, now," Mrs. Plimpton said as she walked over to where I'd left the wagon. "Just think, Molly Harter. What if someone had an emergency and couldn't get through because you and your friend had tied up the line?"

"But, Mrs. Plimpton, my sister—she's—"

"No time to chat, child. Let's just bring this case of cookies in. Then I'll give you a check and you can leave."

"Mrs. Plimpton!" I said, but Mrs. Plimpton ignored me. She was busy pulling me into her store with one hand and hauling the wagonload of cookies with the other.

"Mrs. Plimpton!" I shouted. But at that moment the phone in the Food-a-Rama rang. Mrs. Plimpton dropped my hand and grabbed for the phone on the wall. She began talking a blue streak.

"Edna!" she said. "Edna Ferbish! So nice to hear from you, Edna. It really is. Oh, I can't tell you what a dreadful day I've been having, dear.

"Guess who stopped in today? Mavis Whimple. You remember her, Edna. Great fat cow of a woman. Do you know what she asked me, dear? She asked me if I stocked *diet chocolates*. DIET CHOCOLATES!!! Hmmmmmmph! I told her I don't believe in diet *anything*. Nasty stuff in my book. Nasty.

"Well, do you know that Mavis claims she's lost fifteen pounds in her Pound Whoppers Club? She suggested that *I* join. *Me,* Edna. Well, Edna, you know that I'm not *fat*. Big boned, yes. A tad on the *plump* side, maybe. But *fat?* Well, you can imagine what I told her to—"

"Mrs. Plimpton!"

Mrs. Plimpton frowned and looked over at me.

"Molly," she said coolly, "I am writing your check out right now." She turned back to the phone. "Honestly, Edna," she said. "Children today! No manners. None at all."

At that moment the door to the Food-a-Rama burst

30

open and a policeman with a long, stern face marched in. He was tall and thin and there was a gun on his belt.

Mrs. Plimpton's jaw dropped about a mile.

"What on earth? What—what's—"

"Name's Officer Brenner, ma'am," the policeman said. "We got a call on the emergency phone two stores down. From a kid named Molly Harter. He looked at Janet and me. "Told us a four-year-old was missing. Was it one of you kids who called?"

"It was me, Officer Brenner. I called."

Just then the door to the Food-a-Rama burst open again and two more men walked in. One of them wore shiny, wire-rimmed glasses and was carrying a notepad. The other had a camera slung around his neck by a strap.

"Jennings—Brampton Hills *Herald*," the man with the glasses said. "And this is Quigly—our photographer. We were on our way back to the paper—we just finished writing up a new store opening—but we spotted the police car out front. Anything suspicious going on here?"

"Oh!" Mrs. Plimpton said. "My heart!" And she grabbed at her chest.

"Take it easy, lady," Officer Brenner said. "Hysterics don't help anyone, you know." He turned to the reporter and the photographer. "I'm here following up on a report we got about a missing child." He turned to me. "Now suppose you tell me just what happened, little girl."

I could tell Mrs. Plimpton didn't like the fact that there was a policeman and a reporter in her store. And I could tell she didn't like the way Officer Brenner told her to take it easy. And I could tell that, most of all, she didn't like the fact that everybody was worried about Becka and nobody was worried about *her*.

Mrs. Plimpton really liked people to make a fuss over her. Especially when she was having a heart attack. But

I guess Officer Brenner knew what he was doing. Because Mrs. Plimpton stopped having a heart attack. Instead she plopped down on a stool behind the counter and just scowled at everyone. The photographer, who seemed sort of irritable scowled back at her.

I told Officer Brenner what happened. He nodded and made some notes on a small pad. The reporter listened quietly and he made notes too. The photographer looked bored.

"My partner, Jerry Zalooski, is questioning the store owners next door," the policeman said. "I wonder, Ms. —uh—"

"Plimpton," Mrs. Plimpton said. "*P* as in parfait, *L* as in lamb chops, *I* as—"

"Uh, I get it," Officer Brenner said. "Okay, Ms. Plimpton, did you see anything suspicious on or around four o'clock?"

"Certainly not!" Mrs. Plimpton said. "I never see anything suspicious!"

She said it so huffily that I almost laughed. But I couldn't because it was too serious. I thought of Mom coming home and finding out that Becka was gone.

I think I was about to cry.

Then it happened.

It was this funny feeling inside my head. A feeling like I just *knew*.

"Of-Officer Brenner," I gasped. "I think I know where Becka is. It's—I—just had a flash."

Chapter Five
Big Blimpy Walks Again

Officer Brenner, the reporter, the photographer, and Mrs. Plimpton were all looking at me as if I had just turned into a werewolf or something.

"She—she has ESP," Janet said, trying to explain. That didn't help, because then the four of them turned and looked at *her* as though *she* had turned into a werewolf. I didn't blame them. It did sound odd.

I ran out the door of the Food-a-Rama. Janet, Officer Brenner, Mrs. Plimpton, and the reporter and photographer from the *Herald* followed me out. As quickly as I could I dashed over to the opening in the sewer in front of the sausage shop. Grabbing hold of the railings I bent down over the dark hole and yelled, *"Becka,* are you down there?"

There was no answer.

"Becka," I said, "if you're down there you've got to come up right now..."

Silence.

"Becka?" I said again. I wasn't so sure this time. Maybe, I thought, maybe my flash had been wrong.

There was silence again. Officer Brenner, the men from the newspaper, and Janet had caught up with me. Even Mrs. Plimpton was running to join the crowd around the sewer.

I stared down into the dark hole. I couldn't see anything. A big tear popped of my eye and slid down into the opening.

And then all of a sudden we heard it.

A soft, tiny little voice.

"No," the little voice said.

It sounded far, far away. I couldn't even tell if it was Becka.

"You have to come out," I yelled. "Come on. Come out now."

"No," the voice said. "No. *No. NO.*"

It was Becka down there all right.

Officer Brenner was standing next to me. The reporter and the photographer stood behind him. Officer Brenner picked up his walkie-talkie. He flicked a switch.

"Jerry," he said into the walkie-talkie. "Looks like we found the missing kid. She's in the sewer in front of the sausage shop. I'm going down and get her. She's either lost down there or scared to climb back up."

Officer Brenner handed the walkie-talkie to the reporter and made his way over to the ladder that led down to the sewer.

"Wait," I whispered. "Stop."

"Stop?" Officer Brenner said. He looked at me curiously. "But I'm going to go get your little sister. She's probably scared to death down there."

Officer Brenner was smart. He knew how to work a walkie-talkie. He knew how to stop Mrs. Plimpton from having a heart attack. But he didn't know Becka.

34

"I think I should go down," I said. "If she sees a stranger coming after her she might run further into the sewer."

Officer Brenner seemed to think it over for a moment.

"You might be right," he finally said. "Maybe it would work out better if you went down instead of me. You sure you're not afraid now?"

"Me?" I said. "No, I'm not afraid."

It was only talk. The Parker Avenue sewer was the last place in the world I wanted to go down. The very last place.

Our next-door neighbor, Leroy Conklin, Sammy's older brother, claims he fell down an opening in the Parker Avenue sewer when he was a little kid. He says he was attacked by rats the size of St. Bernards and alligators that were bigger than the rats.

Three of the toes on Leroy's left foot are missing and Leroy claims that's because an alligator chomped them off in the Parker Avenue sewer. He says it bit through his sneakers and everything.

But horrible as the sewer stories were I knew I had to go and get Becka. It wasn't that I was worried about the alligators and giant rats getting her. Becka wasn't the kind of kid who got gotten by anything. What I was worried about was that she might just take off—maybe to catch a pet for herself—and end up in Alaska or someplace.

"Here," Officer Brenner said. He was handing me a flashlight. I clutched it in my hand, took a deep breath, and started down the ladder. When I got to the bottom I had to hold my nose with my free hand. It smelled awful down there!

I looked up. I could see Janet's and Officer Brenner's faces leaning over the sewer opening. They looked far away.

35

I swallowed hard. The smell was terrible. How could Becka stand it? And where was she anyway? I couldn't see her anywhere.

"Becka?" I said, bending down and swiveling the flashlight around in the pipes that led off from the hole I'd climbed down.

The pipes went off in two directions. Even with the flashlight it was hard to see far in either direction.

I started to get scared. What if Becka had decided to run farther away from the opening than she had been? What if I had to walk for miles and miles to find her?

"Becka?" I said again. My voice was a little shaky. It bounced off the tunnel walls. I could hear water dripping and somewhere I heard little feet scurrying. It sounded like rats' feet.

I wanted to drop the flashlight and run back up the ladder. But I knew I couldn't. I stood there, shivering. I didn't know what to do.

Finally I had an idea.

"Becka," I said. "Guess what?"

There was no answer.

"Becka," I said. "I'm a dinosaur. I'm the biggest dinosaur in the ancient jungle. I'm the queen dinosaur."

I heard a giggle!

"See, Becka. Look." I flashed the flashlight on myself as best I could and began to stomp around. I made the same piggy sounds Becka made when she pretended to be a dinosaur.

"Dinosaur," I heard a small voice say. I could tell the way she said it that she thought I was a pretty good dinosaur.

"Right," I said. "Dinosaur. And do you know what the queen of the dinosaurs is going to do?"

"What?" Becka asked. I could tell she liked this game. "What is she going to do? What?" she asked.

"The queen of the dinosaurs is going to climb up the ladder and have her dinner. And do you know what her dinner will be?"

"What?" Becka asked.

"A whole bag of Chocky Chunkas. She's going to eat as many as she wants to."

"YUM!" Becka shouted. This time her voice wasn't soft at all. It was *loud*. I figured she'd gotten pretty hungry hanging around the sewer.

Before I had a chance to ask if there were any other hungry dinosaurs in the sewer, Becka splashed out of one of the pipes and ran into me, grunting and snuffling as loudly as she could.

Part of me wanted to give her a great big hug, and part of me wanted to smack her on the bottom. I couldn't decide which I wanted to do more.

But I couldn't do either. I knew I had to keep snorting and climb up the ladder so that Becka would follow me.

When I finally got to the top of the sewer ladder Officer Brenner gave us a hand. As soon as my feet hit the sidewalk Janet wrinkled up her nose and said, *"Phew!"* And Mrs. Plimpton acted like she would have another heart attack in a minute. I looked down at my sneakers.

Yuck! They were a disaster! A perfectly good pair of Nikes covered with sewer sludge! Icky black and green slime that smelled like rotten eggs mixed up with old fish heads and cod-liver oil. It was the worst.

At least I thought it was until Officer Brenner pulled Becka out. The photographer aimed his camera at me and at Becka behind me and snapped away. I turned around, took one look at her, and gasped.

Becka was covered head-to-toe with slimy sewer gunk. Even her ponytails.

"Becka!" I said. "What did you do down there?"

"I played dinosaur," Becka said, with a satisfied grin.

37

I groaned.

"You mean you rolled around in all that dirt and gunk?"

Becka ignored me.

"Where's the cookies?" she said. "You said there were cookies."

I looked at her hands. They were black and green.

"Becka Harter, you're not eating a thing till you get home and clean up."

"We'll help you get her home," Officer Brenner said. "We can wrap her in a blanket."

"I want *COOKIES*," Becka screamed.

Everyone ignored her.

I turned to Mrs. Plimpton. I wanted to tell her about the accident with the cookies. Mrs. Plimpton was holding her heart with one hand and fanning her nose with the other.

"My stars," she was muttering. "My stars."

"Mrs. Plimpton?" I began.

"What?" she said. "What is it?"

She sounded kind of edgy. I didn't blame her. I knew reporters and photographers and policemen probably didn't burst into her store every day.

"I—I wanted to tell you that—"

But I couldn't finish. Becka looked up at Mrs. Plimpton the minute I started to speak. I guess she'd forgotten about getting a snack for herself just then, because she had this adoring expression all over her dirty face.

I could tell she really liked Mrs. Plimpton. For a minute I was so surprised I couldn't think. Then, by the time I figured out what was going to happen, it was too late.

Before I could stop her Becka ran over to Mrs. Plimpton, wrapped her arms as far around her as they would go, and gave her a big, slime-covered hug!

"Big Blimpy!" Becka yelled. "Bi-i-i-ig Blimpy!"

38

Mrs. Plimpton's eyes became as small and hard as raisins. Officer Brenner's mouth and nose twitched and twitched and I thought he was going to sneeze. The photographer was grinning from ear to ear and the reporter was pretending to cough, but really he was laughing behind his hand. Janet was standing there trying to keep her eyes on my sneakers. I wanted to disappear back down the sewer pipe.

Finally Officer Brenner managed to peel Becka off Mrs. Plimpton and wrap her in a blanket. Mrs. Plimpton went off in a huff, and the photographer made a motion to the reporter, Mr. Jennings, as though he were ready to leave. Mr. Jennings nodded. Before he left with the photographer though, he put his hand on my shoulder and patted it.

"Well, Miss Harter, I'd say Brampton Hills has a new heroine."

I knew he was just trying to be nice, but I could feel my cheeks turn hot and pink.

Officer Brenner drove us home. The sun was going down. Big storm clouds looked like gray cotton balls someone had stuck onto the sky. Becka and I sat in the backseat. Janet sat in front. I couldn't see her face.

When we got to my house Janet ran inside to get her bookbag. She came back and sat down in the front seat again. Just before I got out she turned around and gave me a big grin.

"Molly," she whispered, "this was the most fun I've ever had."

I stared at her. Was she being sarcastic or what? I wondered.

"Riding in a police car," Janet said, "and being interviewed by a reporter, and you having ESP after all— wow!"

Just then Mom's station wagon came to a stop in front

of our house. Mom saw the police car in our driveway, tumbled out of her wagon, and ran toward us.

Officer Brenner nodded politely at Mom. Mom's eyes flicked past Officer Brenner, past me, and into the backseat of the police car. In the backseat Mom saw a small kid with a very dirty face who was rolled up in a blanket like a sausage.

Officer Brenner started to tell Mom what had happened. The next thing I knew I heard Mom, who never yells, yell, *"In the sewer! My children were in the sewer!"*

Mom isn't a neatness freak or anything like that. But she is a pretty clean person. I think the idea of the two of us stomping around in sewer sludge was a little much for her to take.

"Oh, my darlings," she yelled. "Oh, my poor sweets."

Officer Brenner opened the door to let Becka out. As soon as she wriggled out of the car, Mom reached over to grab her. And as soon as she hugged her, she began to gasp and choke. Becka's blanket fell off and she stood there, smiling up at Mom and looking like the Creature from the Black Lagoon.

"It's okay, Mom," I said. "It's just some dirt and slime, that's all."

Mom's shoulders were hunched up behind her, the way they always got when she was really worried about something. She turned to Officer Brenner. "Should I— should I take her to the hospital? All those germs . . ."

"No, ma'am. I checked with the emergency medicos on our police line and they said that it was only a drainage sewer and that all she really needs is a good bath."

Mom's shoulders unhunched a little.

"Oh, *Becka,*" Mom said.

Becka gave Mom a big grin. Her open mouth was like

a white half-moon glowing in the middle of her dirty face.

Becka can get away with a lot when she gives Mom her big grin. But that's when she doesn't smell like the Parker Avenue sewer. Mom didn't crack a smile at all.

"Young lady," she said, "you are marching into that house and you are taking a good long soak in the tub."

I knew from the way Mom said it that Becka wasn't going to get out of the tub until she'd pruned up all over.

Officer Brenner took down some information, tipped his cap at Mom, and climbed back into the car.

"Well, young lady," he said, speaking to me before he drove off, "I guess tomorrow you'll be famous."

"Huh?" I said.

"The reporter from the *Herald*," Officer Brenner explained. "The way he was taking notes, I'm pretty sure that by tomorrow morning everyone in Brampton Hills will be reading about the girl who saved her sister from the sewer."

Chapter Six
Happy Birthday, Clare

When I came down to breakfast the morning after Officer Brenner dropped us off at home, Nikki was sitting at the kitchen table, her eyes scanning the morning paper. Becka sat next to her, a big proud grin on her face.

Nikki had come home late last night from her girlfriend's. I guess Mom hadn't had a chance to tell her what had happened to Becka and me on Parker Avenue.

I leaned over Nikki's shoulder and looked at the article she was reading in the *Herald*. Splashed on page one was the picture of Becka and me the photographer from the paper had snapped yesterday—just as we were coming out of the sewer. The headline next to the picture read: GIRL ACTS LIKE DINOSAUR/ SAVES SIS FROM SEWER.

"Molly," Becka said proudly, "we're *famous*."

Nikki turned to me. "Molly, couldn't you have kept a better eye on her? I can't wait to hear what my friends at school have to say about me having two sisters who like to hang out in the Parker Avenue sewer."

She picked up a piece of toast and started to butter it.

"Where's Mom?" I asked. "Did she see the paper?"

"She's in the pantry getting some napkins," Nikki said. "And, yeah, she saw the paper."

"She thought it was *GREAT!*" Becka shouted.

She put the empty plastic napkin holder on her nose and tried to balance it. It clattered to the table and just missed knocking over the marmalade jar.

"She thought it was *okay,*" Nikki whispered to me in a soft voice so that Becka couldn't hear, "but don't mention it to her, Molly. I think she's worried about something today."

Nikki was right. Mom came back into the kitchen with a stack of paper napkins in her hand. She stuck the napkins into the plastic holder, sat down, and poured herself a cup of coffee.

"Good morning, Mom," I said.

"Hmmmm? Oh, good morning, dear," Mom said.

I waited for her to say something about the story in the *Herald*. But Mom didn't say anything about it. Mom didn't seem to be thinking about the story in the *Herald* at all. She *was* worried about something. I wondered what. I knew it couldn't be the story in the paper. Nikki asked the question before I could.

"Mom," Nikki said, "did Mr. Glemp decide to buy our cookies?"

Mom sighed.

"No, he didn't, dear," she said quietly. "As a matter of fact, he wouldn't even sample my cookies. He said the same thing all the other supermarket managers did, that Farmer Fred's had a good enough assortment of chocolate-chip cookies for the moment."

43

"But, Mom, that's unfair," I said. "Your cookies aren't just like everybody else's. They're the best."

Mom sighed again.

"You think so," she said, "and I think so—but, unfortunately, Mr. Glemp doesn't think so."

"He didn't even *try* them?" Nikki asked.

"No. He said it didn't matter what my cookies tasted like. He just wasn't interested."

A faraway rumbling, chugging sound was getting louder and louder. It was Nikki's bus.

Nikki gulped down her orange juice and got up.

"What a crumb!" she said. She grabbed her books and ran out the door.

As the door closed behind Nikki the kitchen phone rang. Mom picked it up. She didn't even have a chance to say hello. Whoever was on the other end of the line was yelling so loudly I could hear it halfway across the kitchen.

"What?" Mom said. "Oh, no. Oh, that's terrible. Really terrible. Well, of course not. No, of course I don't expect you to pay for them. But I do wish you'd reconsider closing your account with us, Aggie."

There was a loud click. Mom stared at the receiver for a minute, then hung it up on its hook. She looked at me with a puzzled expression on her face.

"All right, Molly," she said, "now suppose you tell me what on earth happened to that case of Chocky Chunkas I sent over to the Food-a-Rama last night?"

"Oh!" I said. With all the excitement going on—the police and the reporter and photographer—I'd forgotten all about Becka sitting on the cookies.

I told Mom what had happened. While I was talking Becka munched away on her toast and marmalade. When I got to the part about Becka giving Mrs. Plimpton a slimy hug and calling her Big Blimpy, Becka stopped munching for a minute, looked up, and said, "I hugged her hard."

Mom let out a groan.

"Well," Mom said as she watched Becka reach over and help herself to another piece of toast, "I guess I'll just have to go and talk to Aggie when she's calmed down. Maybe she'll change her mind."

She frowned. "I hope that she does. Just now we need every account we can get."

I was about to get up and leave for school when the phone rang again. Mom was just answering it as I grabbed my bookbag and left the house. Maybe it was Mrs. Plimpton calling back to apologize, I thought as I walked to school. I realized that Mom hadn't said anything to me about my being in the Brampton Hills *Herald*. I told myself she had a lot on her mind. Still, I felt kind of down.

It didn't help when I reached the corner of Morningside Street, where I had to pass the Digbert Brothers Funeral Home. Clare and Norma popped out of the funeral home and started walking behind me. They were walking to school together, as usual lately. Clare was carrying a big shopping bag. That's when I remembered that her birthday was in November.

Clare's dad was the manager of the Parker Avenue Farmer Fred's. Whenever Clare had a birthday she always brought free samples of new products from the store as treats. The treats weren't always too exciting. One year everybody had gotten a lint brush. Another time we'd all gotten one unbreakable trash bag apiece.

For about a minute Clare and Norma just kept following me. Then Norma said in a loud voice, "I read the paper today, Clare. How about you?"

I gritted my teeth together and waited. But Clare didn't say anything. I was a little surprised.

45

I turned around and looked at her. When she saw me look at her she looked away, but she'd let her mouth fall a little open. That was what Clare did when she felt funny about something.

"The school's in the other direction, Molly," Norma said, "so what are you looking at?"

"Not at your face," I said. "I don't want my watch to stop."

Norma's mouth twisted.

"Sewer rat," she hissed.

I turned back around and closed the distance between the school and myself. I walked faster than I usually do.

The first thing Mrs. Marnock did that morning was to pass around the Brampton Hills *Herald* and make sure everyone got to see the picture of Becka and me on the front page.

Most of the kids thought the sewer story was neat, just like Mrs. Marnock did. Some of them didn't.

Halfway into the morning, just after Mrs. Marnock left the room for a few minutes to see the language arts teacher about borrowing a projector, I had to pass Norma's desk to get to the pencil sharpener. As I walked by her, Norma made this loud choking noise. "Aaagh," she gasped, "those sewer fumes. Yuck!" Eddie Kleeg chimed in. "Yeah, what're you wearing, Molly? Parker Avenue Perfume? Chanel Number Sewer?"

Some of the kids laughed. Some of them started holding their noses and making gasping sounds. It was really hard, but I tried to ignore it.

I was glad when Mrs. Marnock got back.

Mrs. Marnock told Clare to go ahead and give out her birthday treats.

Norma helped Clare give out the treats. Since I sat in the first seat in the first row I was the first kid to get the

46

treat. I stared at the cube of shiny yellowy-green stuff wrapped in cellophane that Clare dropped onto my desk.

"I hope you enjoy these treats," Clare was saying. She wasn't talking to me. She was talking to the whole class. As usual when she gave out free samples from her dad's store, she managed to sound a little bit like a commercial.

"This health-food candy is called Jolly Jelly. It's a product my dad will soon be selling in the gourmet treats section of the Farmer Fred he manages." Clare was really proud of the fact that her dad was a supermarket manager. She mentioned it every chance she got.

I looked at the candy again. It looked gross. But I could hear the other kids tearing at the cellophane. Mrs. Marnock, who'd gotten her treat before me, was taking a bite.

Clare kept on talking about how great the candy was.

"Jolly Jelly," she said, "is made with 100 percent pure natural ingredients. Besides being delicious, Jolly Jelly has more vitamins and minerals than broccoli. It's a scientifically formulated dessert food. It was invented by a marine biologist from Boston and it's unique because it's the first candy that is 95 percent algae."

All of a sudden the cellophane wrappers stopped crinkling.

I looked over at Mrs. Marnock. She stopped chewing. Her lips puckered up and her face turned very pink. She got up quickly and mumbled, "Excoos me, children," and then rushed out the door. Clare watched her leave with an annoyed expression on her face.

I got curious. I opened the package and took a tiny bite of the jelly. It tasted so awful I wanted to spit it out. It was kind of like I imagined dirty socks would taste if you mixed them up with sugar syrup and made jelly out of them.

Just then Mrs. Marnock came back into the room. She looked sort of funny, the way Mom looks sometimes when she finds out that Becka has thrown oatmeal into the goldfish bowl or locked the baby-sitter in the cellar. But she spoke in a nice pleasant voice when she told us we could either eat our treats or put them away for later.

The whole class stuck their Jolly Jellies into their desks. Except for Randy Bartell. He ate his.

That didn't say too much for the candies. Randy Bartell would eat anything. Last year there had even been a rumor going around the fourth grade that he'd eaten the frog Miss Linton had brought in for the science class to study. Randy denied it but maybe it was true because after Kermit disappeared Miss Linton made sure she never left Randy alone with the salamander or the guinea pig.

I looked over at Clare. I could tell she was in a bad mood because nobody was crazy about her Jolly Jellies. Still, I didn't feel sorry for her. What can you expect if you serve algae as a birthday treat?

The lunch bell finally rang and Mrs. Marnock got ready to leave for the teachers' lounge while we pulled our lunch bags out of our desks and backpacks. Before she left she told us that Mrs. Keller was sick and wouldn't be in to watch us as usual.

Mrs. Keller was the fifth-grade lunch mother. She came to supervise our room at lunchtime.

Later I decided it was too bad Mrs. Keller wasn't able to make it the day Clare gave out her birthday treats, because if she had maybe I wouldn't have ended up in the principal's office.

Chapter Seven
The Jolly Jelly War

It all started about two seconds after Mrs. Marnock left the classroom. I was walking up to the front of the room to get my carton of milk from the bin on Mrs. Marnock's desk when suddenly I heard a great big "Hey!" from the back of the classroom.

I turned and took a look. It was Eddie Kleeg. He was holding something between his stretched-out hands. It looked like a giant green rubber band.

"Hey!" Eddie said again. "This stuff stretches."

It was the Jolly Jelly.

Of course, about six seconds later all the kids were digging through their desks and pulling out their packages of Jolly Jelly.

"Gosh," Kevin Sanders said. "It feels just like rubber cement."

I could tell Clare was mad. She was staring at Kevin and her face was a splotchy red. I guess it would be kind of irritating to hear someone call your birthday treat rubber cement.

"Hey!" Alex Stern said. "Let's throw it. Maybe it bounces."

Alex was the best pitcher in the Brampton Hills Little League. He squished his Jolly Jelly into a glob, wound up his arm, and threw it at the floor. It stuck there like glue.

"Aw, geez," Alex said.

"Hey," Derek Greener said. "Look at this." Everyone turned and stared where he was pointing. Hanging from one of the flourescent lights on the ceiling was a long green string of stuff.

"Wow! This stuff is awesome," Derek shouted. "It sticks and stretches. *Neat-o.*"

Naturally, it didn't take too long before there were a dozen more strings of Jolly Jelly hanging from the ceiling. Almost all the boys, except for Randy Bartell and Tim Sparley, who wanted to be a minister when he grew up, were throwing their treats around. A few of the girls were too. Randy Bartell begged me for my Jolly Jelly. He was pretty upset because he'd eaten his. I wouldn't give it to him. I didn't want to add to the mess on the ceiling. Besides, I was beginning to feel a tiny bit sorry for Clare.

I was just standing there, at Mrs. Marnock's desk, with my milk carton in my hand, watching all the crazy stuff going on when all of a sudden: splat! A piece of Jolly Jelly landed on my arm. It kind of surprised me. I dropped my carton of milk. Luckily it wasn't opened, so it didn't spill. I bent down to pick it up when—splat!—another piece of Jolly Jelly hit me on my other arm. I turned in the direction the jelly came from. Norma Digbert was smiling a mean smile.

Just then a blob of Jolly Jelly from the ceiling worked

loose and fell on the floor about a foot away from me. If Norma hadn't had such a snotty look on her face maybe I wouldn't have done what I did. But she did have a snotty look on her face, and I didn't even think about what I was doing. I just scooped up the jelly that had fallen and lobbed it over at her. Splat! It landed on her shoulder. Norma turned so red she was almost purple.

Splat! Splat! Splat! The jellies kept falling from the ceiling. As fast as they fell kids scooped them up and threw them around. Jolly Jelly was whizzing through the air in all directions.

Ducking the wads of Jolly Jelly, I tried to walk back to my seat without getting hit. But just as I sat down I got splatted by another glob, this time on my shoulder.

Then another.

I turned around. Sure enough, Norma Digbert was grabbing jelly globs and throwing them my way as fast as she could.

I got up slowly and walked over to her desk.

"Norma Digbert," I said.

For a while Norma just stared at me, her eyes small and hard. I stared back.

Meanwhile the whole class was going crazy. Jellies were whizzing through the air. Left and right, faster and faster. Norma and I kept staring at each other.

"Cut it out," I said.

"Fat chance," Norma said. She was bending down to scoop up another glob of jelly to throw.

I went back to my desk, grabbed my milk carton, and walked back to where Norma was sitting. It took me about one second to open my milk carton and about a half a second to dump it over Norma's head.

Norma screamed—and that's when Mrs. Marnock came in.

The next thing I knew the two of us—Norma and I—were sitting in the principal's office.

Mr. Lewis gave us a long lecture about controlling ourselves. He told us we each had to write a 500-word essay on the subject. He said if we ever came into his office again for losing control of ourselves that he'd have to call our parents in.

Finally he said we could go. After we got out of Mr. Lewis's office, Norma grabbed me. Her fingers felt like steel pins sinking into my arm.

"You think you're smart, don't you?" she said.

"Let go," I said. I yanked my arm away.

Norma put her hands on her hips and squinted at me.

"You think you're just the greatest, don't you, Molly Harter? You think you can get away with anything."

I thought it sounded an awful lot as though Norma were talking about herself. I also thought Norma was pretty dumb, trying to pick another fight with me right outside Mr. Lewis's office. I turned my back on her and started walking back to the classroom. Before I'd gotten a step away from her, Norma ran and stood in front of me, blocking my path. Her face was about a foot away from mine. It was all white and the eyes in the middle of it were boiling mad. Even the curls of her blond hair, which were wisping away from her face, looked angry.

"What is your problem, Norma?" I said. I was trying hard to keep from shouting.

Norma's eyes narrowed into mean little slits.

"I don't care if Uncle John does have a date with your mother this Saturday," Norma hissed. "Once I tell him what you're like, I'll bet you anything he won't ask her out again."

Date? Saturday? What was she talking about?

"Norma Digbert, are you crazy? My mother would never date your uncle."

The angry line that was Norma's mouth got even thinner. For a long moment she just stared at me.

Finally she said, "Well, it looks like you've got a lot to learn."

Then she turned around and walked away.

That afternoon, during art class, while everyone else was having a great time making papier-mâché turkeys and horns of plenty, Mrs. Marnock made the two of us, Norma and me, go around the classroom with a roll of paper towels and a spray bottle of cleaner and wipe up all the splotches left by the Jolly Jelly. After school, she made us wait by her desk until everyone had left.

For a minute I was afraid she was going to tell us to get a ladder and clean the ceiling too, but she didn't. She told us that Mr. Henly, the school janitor, would do it. And then she gave us a long talk about how old Mr. Henly was, and about how hard it was going to be for him to have to climb up a ladder to do the cleaning. I don't know how Norma felt, but I felt pretty bad.

Mrs. Marnock was good at making you feel guilty. She wasn't being too fair though, because it was Eddie Kleeg and Kevin Sanders and Derek Greener who had started throwing the globs of Jolly Jelly around. And it was Norma who had started the fight with me.

Teachers are like that. They can leave the room and while they're gone the whole class can go wild and act crazy. But the only people who get the lecture and the punishment are the ones they catch red-handed.

Finally we got to leave the classroom. Norma stomped off in a huff, beating me to the exit door. The corridor had that funny, lonely, after-school feeling. It was cool and sunshiny outside, and at the bottom of the steps Janet was leaning against the school building. She was bouncing a pink rubber ball in a bored way.

"Hi," I said, "How come you're still hanging around school?"

"I wasn't in any big rush," she said, tossing the ball at me. I caught it and threw it back. We kept pitching it back and forth.

After a while we started throwing it up in higher and higher arches. That made it harder to catch. Then Janet called the new pitch the Jolly Jelly throw and that made us both start giggling so hard we couldn't concentrate on catching anymore. Janet stuck the ball in her knapsack and we started walking home.

"What happened in Mr. Lewis's office?" Janet asked.

I told her about the essay he'd assigned us, and then I told her about what Norma had said about her uncle dating my mom.

"Your mom and Mr. Digbert?" Janet said. She sounded as though she couldn't believe it.

"Norma's a liar," I said. "She's a big fat liar."

I thought about it. Mom and Mr. Digbert dating. Yuck!

"But, Molly," Janet said, "what if—"

Janet didn't finish the sentence. She didn't have to. My mind finished it for her: I didn't want to think it, but I did: What if—what if it were true? What if mom and Mr. Digbert did have a date on Saturday? What if they started dating and fell in love? What if they started dating and fell in love and got married, and—I started shaking—and Mr. Digbert became my stepdad?

Chapter Eight
The Count Pays a Call

When I yanked open the door to our house, a chocolaty smell hit my nose. I slammed my books down onto the hallway table and skimmed the stairs to the basement.

Mom was pulling trays of cookies out of the oven.

"Mom," I said, panting, *"is it true?"*

"Is what true, Molly?"

"Is it true that you're *dating* him?"

Mom blinked at me.

"Him?" she said. "Who do you mean?"

"Oh, Mom, you know who I mean. Mr. Digbert."

Mom pulled the last tray out of the oven and set it on a table to cool. Then she climbed up on the tall stool that stood next to the long table where she mixed and worked with the cookie dough.

"Molly," she said, "John Digbert and I are just friends."

"Then—then Norma was lying about your dating him?"

"Molly," Mom said slowly, "I didn't say I wouldn't go out with John. I just said we're only friends."

"But, Mom, Mr. Digbert? You *wouldn't*. You just *couldn't*. You just—"

"And why not?" Mom asked.

"Because," I said.

Mom's voice was soft, but I could tell she meant business.

"'Because' doesn't seem like much of a reason."

"Oh, Mom, you just c-c-can't," I spluttered. "I hate Norma Digbert, and, besides that, Mr. Digbert is a—is a—*mortician.*"

"Gosh," Mom said, "you make that sound like something terrible."

"Mom," I shouted, "it's not just that he's an undertaker. It's—well, it's *him*. He's so—so *creepy*."

Mom gave me the same kind of look she used to give me when I was little and I'd told her a whopper.

"Oh, Molly," she said, "I'll admit that John Digbert is a bit stuffy. But we're just going golfing on Saturday, that's all. Besides, I suspect that underneath the fussy exterior, down where it really counts, he's basically a warm, caring person."

I didn't. I suspected that underneath the fussy exterior, down where it really counted, Mr. Digbert was basically an iceberg.

"And, besides that," Mom went on, "he's hardworking and responsible and—"

Just then our neighbor's collie started barking up a storm. I looked at my Star Wars watch. It was almost four o'clock. Sandy was probably barking at the mailman.

I didn't want to hear any more about how great Mr.

Digbert was so I excused myself and ran to get the mail. It was all for Mom except for a *Cricket* magazine. That was for me.

I tossed the *Cricket* on the hall table on top of my books and carried the rest of the mail down to Mom. Mom finished setting the switches on the mixer and then took the stack of mail I handed her and flipped through it with a sad expression on her face.

"Oh, dear," she said. She sounded tired.

"Are they all bills, Mom?"

Mom nodded.

I wanted to ask her if she'd had a chance to talk Mrs. Plimpton into buying Chocky Chunkas for the Food-a-Rama again. But just then the mixer timer went off. Mom went over to the dough table and I could tell she didn't want me to ask her any more questions.

When Nikki got home from her swim team practice I asked her if she knew anything about what had happened between Mom and Mrs. Plimpton.

"Uh-huh," Nikki said. "Mom told me what happened. So I went over there after school and apologized for you and Becka. Mrs. Plimpton's going to buy Mom's cookies again."

"Oh," I said.

I went out into the backyard. It was empty. I sat on the edge of Becka's sandbox and swirled sand through my fingers. Why hadn't I thought of going to Mrs. Plimpton and apologizing? Why was Nikki the one who did everything right?

I had trouble falling asleep that night. I was still awake when Mom called Grandma Mundy on the phone. I don't think she knew I could hear her.

"Yes, it is serious, Mother," Mom said. "If I don't start selling a few hundred more cases of cookies a week before the end of this month, I just won't have enough

57

cash flow to keep the business going. I—I'll have to file for bankruptcy.

"If only," Mom sighed, "I'd had better luck with Fred Glemp. A big account like Farmer Fred's could have gotten us into the black right now."

Mom talked some more.

But I didn't hear the rest of the conversation too clearly. I kept thinking about what Mom had said about the cookie business. And I kept thinking about school, and how Clare wasn't my best friend or even my friend at all this year and how Norma hated me. And, most of all, I thought about Mom going out with Mr. Digbert.

Finally, I fell asleep. I had a crazy dream. I dreamed bags and bags of Mom's cookies came to life. They turned into little cookie people with arms and hands and legs. There were thousands of them. And they were running after me. They chased me up Morningside Street. They chased me and chased me until I ended up running into the Digbert Brothers Funeral Home to hide. I slammed the door on them and locked it. For a minute I thought I was safe.

But just then Mr. Digbert came down the lobby stairs. He was dressed in his golfing clothes. And on top of his black shirt and shorts he was wearing a long black cape with a red silk lining. The cape had a tall stiff collar that rose up around his neck. A couple of bats were circling around his head.

He heard the cookie people knocking on the door. He walked to the door and opened it. The cookies had disappeared. Instead, just outside the door, there was this giant golf ball. It was a golf ball bigger than an elephant.

Norma appeared behind the golf ball. She was ten feet tall and she was holding a gigantic golf club. She swung it at the gigantic ball. It started rolling toward me . . .

Saturday morning Janet invited me over to her house. We played Scrabble for a while. Then we watched Muffin, Janet's hamster, run around on his exercise wheel and stuff his cheeks with hamster feed. Then we went roller skating in front of Janet's house. It was fun.

When I got back home Mom was getting ready for her golf date with Mr. Digbert. She was in the bathroom combing her hair in front of the mirror and humming. I wanted to throw up.

I thought about the horrible possibilities.

Mom and Mr. Digbert: They would go out. They'd have a great time. Mr. Digbert would call Mom up for another date. Then another. And another. Then they'd get engaged. And—before I knew what was happening —Norma Digbert would be my *cousin,* and Mom and Nikki and Becka and I would have to go and live with the rest of the Digberts in the House of Formaldehyde.

At 1:30 the doorbell rang.

"Well, aren't you going to answer it, Molly?" Mom asked.

She was dabbing cologne behind her ears.

It's terrible being a kid, I thought. The doorbell rings and if your Mom tells you to, you have to go answer it, even if Count Dracula is on the other side.

I opened the door and there he was: Mr. Digbert. His golf slacks and golf shirt were black, just like in my dream. I stared hard at the little embroidered design on his chest pocket. At first I thought that maybe it was a tiny coffin or something. But it wasn't. It was only an alligator.

Mr. Digbert smiled at me. It was a really fakey sort of smile. I didn't even try to smile back at him. I just opened the door and told him to come in.

"Hello, John," Mom said as she walked into the

foyer. "I'm afraid we're going to have to wait a while before we can leave. Aggie Plimpton from the Food-a-Rama just called. She's going to stop by and pick up a carton of cookies. She said she'd be here within half an hour. I hope you don't mind. We can sit down while we're waiting and have some coffee."

Chapter Nine
A Guest in the House

Ten minutes later Mom and Mr. Digbert were sitting on the living room couch and drinking coffee. I hung around the living room with them. I sat down in one of the chairs and pretended to read a *Time* magazine.

Pretty soon Becka stomped in from where she was playing in the backyard. When she spotted Mr. Digbert she walked over to the archway to the living room and just stood there with her hands on her hips, staring at him. She stood there for a long time.

"Uh, Becka," Mom said, "wouldn't you like to go outside and play some more, sweetheart? I think I see Sammy Conklin riding his tricycle out front."

Becka shook her head. She kept on staring at Mr. Digbert. Mom looked at me.

"Uh, c'mon, Becka," I said, standing up and putting the magazine back down on the coffee table, "let's go to the rec room and find that dinosaur story you like. Maybe you'd like to hear it again, huh?"

Becka shook her head no. She walked over to Mr. Digbert. She walked up so near to him that she was almost standing on his toes.

All of a sudden Becka put her hands on his knees and pushed her face up to his so that her nose almost bumped into Mr. Digbert's.

Mr. Digbert looked startled. His coffee cup rattled in its saucer a little.

"Becka," Mom said, and I noticed her voice was extra firm, "Mr. Digbert is a guest in our house."

But Becka was too young to understand about guests, and how you're supposed to be polite to people who visit in your house. She had this funny look on her face. Personally I was pretty sure she had the right attitude about Mr. Digbert. But I knew Mom didn't think so.

"C'mon, Becka," I said, taking her by the hand and yanking her away from where she was standing. "C'mon. Let's see if there's a good show on TV. I'll make us some popcorn."

Becka let me pull her over to the rec room. I was lucky. The *Bill the Clown Show* was on TV. Becka liked the *Bill the Clown Show*. Maybe that was because the show was taped in Detroit, which wasn't too far from Brampton Hills, so Becka had seen Bill the Clown in lots of parades and festivals on Parker Avenue.

Becka sat down cross-legged on the floor, wrapped her arms around her knees, and hugged them tight. She watched the show. She wasn't too happy though. I could tell, because every few minutes she'd turn around and look through the rec room door into the living room and scowl at Mr. Digbert.

I went to the kitchen and popped some popcorn in the microwave. I poured it into a bowl, carried it to the rec room, and set it down next to Becka and me. I didn't eat

62

much though. Mr. Digbert was sitting in our living room, and that sort of took my appetite away.

Becka didn't eat much either. She nibbled on a few pieces and then turned, frowning, and looked at me.

"Molly," she said, "I don't like him."

She was staring out the rec room door. You could see the backs of Mr. Digbert's and Mom's heads over the couch.

"Becka," I whispered, "I don't like him either, but we can't do anything about it."

"*Look,*" Becka whispered. Her eyes and mouth were opened wide.

I looked back into the living room. Mr. Digbert had put his arm around Mom's shoulder! I wished Mrs. Plimpton would hurry up.

After that we didn't touch the popcorn. It just sat there while we watched TV.

The *Bill the Clown Show* was pretty dumb, but watching it was better than thinking about Mom sitting in the living room with Mr. Digbert's arm around her shoulders.

Bill the Clown was, as usual, running a contest. About ten of the kids in his studio audience got called from their seats. They had to balance an orange on their heads for as long as they could. Bill the Clown laughed a lot. He kept laughing when the oranges fell off the kids' heads.

Finally only one kid was left with an orange on his head. The big winner. Bill the Clown gave him his prize: a Bill the Clown doll.

Then Bill the Clown stuck his face up close to the TV camera and yelled: "Hello out there, all of you kids at home. Guess what? *You're* going to get a chance to see Bill the Clown—that's me!—IN PERSON! That's right! *You* can see *ME* in person. *WOW!!!*

63

"All you have to do is this: Come down to the Brampton Hills Mall for the city's Fiftieth Anniversary Party NEXT SATURDAY! That's right, boys and girls, the city of Brampton Hills is FIFTY years old! And to help celebrate I'LL BE THERE! And so will my good buddy, the mayor of Brampton Hills, Mr. Henry Cosgill! You can meet him too—a real live mayor!

"You know, boys and girls, maybe this would be a good time for you to tell your moms and dads that the Brampton Hills Mall has just been completely modernized. Do you know what that means? It means that the buildings have all been ROOFED OVER! Yes, the mall is now ENCLOSED! And that makes it an even more convenient place for your mom and dad to shop!

"*And*, last but not least, to help us celebrate this FANTASTIC EVENT, all of you out there who enjoy movies will be able to meet: LORETTA LORNE!!! That's RIGHT! You heard me CORRECTLY! LORETTA LORNE!!! Our own hometown girl who is now a world-famous star of stage, screen, and television!!!

"Miss Lorne, who was born and raised in Brampton Hills, is coming back to her hometown to help it celebrate its birthday! So YOU be there too! That's Saturday morning starting at ten, at the BRAMPTON HILLS MALL!"

The camera closed in on Bill the Clown's big grinning mouth. Then Bill the Clown faded away and a commercial for Crunchy Sweeties cereal came on. When that ended, another commercial came on. I hadn't seen the second commercial before. It was for Jolly Jelly. All of a sudden loud music filled the room:

J is for Jolly,
J is for Jelly:

64

J, J, J.
Hey, hey, hey.
Jolly Jelly,
Jolly Jelly,
Jolly Jelly.
Yay!

I stared at the TV. I couldn't believe it. A dancer dressed up as a big Jolly Jelly bar was doing a tap dance around a gigantic life preserver.

The song went on:

> Food from the sea,
> For you and for me.
> Good for you,
> Tasty too:
> Jolly Jelly,
> Jolly Jelly,
> Jolly Jelly.
> Yay!

Suddenly I felt really angry. It just didn't seem fair. Here was this terrible product and people were probably going to buy it anyway—just because there was a commercial for it with someone dancing around in a dumb costume. And Mom, who made the best cookies in the world, was about to go out of business.

If only, I thought, Mom could have put a commercial for Chocky Chunkas on TV. Then people would know how great they were and buy them.

"Molly," Becka said, *"look!"*

I turned around. Mr. Digbert still had his arm around Mom. But now it looked as if he was sitting *even closer* to her on the couch.

Becka stood up. She picked up the bowl of popcorn.

65

She started walking toward the living room with it. *Wow!* I thought. Becka's smarter than I realized. She's going to try to distract Mr. Digbert's attention from Mom by offering him some popcorn.

But it was funny how she was walking over to where he was sitting with Mom. She was tiptoeing on her sneakers, the way she walked when she was pretending to be a ballerina.

Even funnier than that, when she reached where Mom and Mr. Digbert were sitting, instead of circling around the sofa with the bowl of popcorn held out in front of her, she just stopped, lifted the bowl up high, and . . .

"Becka!" I yelled.

It was too late.

The warm buttery popcorn was showering down over Mr. Digbert's head like crunchy snow falling.

"Wh-wh-wha!" Mr. Digbert said, jumping up. Popcorn puffs were stuck in his hair and crammed in the collar of his black golf shirt.

"Becka!" Mom said.

"Well!" Mr. Digbert said.

"Becka, I think you should apologize," Mom said. "At once."

Becka scowled at Mr. Digbert. She didn't say a word.

And then, while Mr. Digbert kept trying to shake popcorn out of his hair and his clothes, Mom gave *me* a long lecture. Mostly it was about how I should have kept a better eye on Becka.

I didn't say anything. I just kept watching Mr. Digbert pulling puffs of popped corn out of his hair and off his shirt. I was enjoying the sight so much I was almost sorry when Mrs. Plimpton picked up her cookies and Mom and Mr. Digbert left for the golf course.

Chapter Ten
The Worst Day Ever

All that weekend I kept trying to think of ways to help Mom with her cookie business. But I didn't come up with anything. I guess I was still thinking hard Monday morning at school as I walked down the corridor to Room 202 because I didn't see Norma coming toward me in the hallway until it was too late.

I just heard this loud "Hey!" and the next thing I knew books, lunches, gym bags, and something that made a crashing, tinkling sound were flying all over the place.

Norma propped herself up on her elbows and glared at me.

"Molly Harter," Norma yelled, "you did that on purpose. You did it on purpose. You wrecked it. You wrecked my science project. Now look at it. Just look."

I looked. In the middle of the corridor, along with our lunches and books and gym bags, there was a pile of wood and sand and glass. Little black specks were wriggling all over the pile.

"My ant farm!" Norma yelled. "You smashed it. It's ruined. All my ants are escaping. And they'll probably die! You—you ant murderer!"

It was embarrassing, being accused of being an ant murderer in front of the whole school. Norma had a voice like a loudspeaker. Mrs. Marnock came out into the hallway and calmed Norma down. She told her that she'd get a credit for effort since the ant farm had broken by accident. And she told her that once we swept them up and let them loose on the playground they'd probably be a lot happier anyway.

At recess that morning, it was sunny out, so Mrs. Marnock let us go out on the playground. Norma got into a huddle with Jackie and Carrie and Clare. The four of them were looking over at me.

I waited. I knew something was going to happen. Something bad.

It did.

Norma and Jackie and Carrie and Clare got into a line, linked hands, and did a cheer. It was a loud cheer and everyone on the playground could hear it.

> " 'M' is for Marbles,
>   (Hers are loose).
> 'O' is for Odd,
>   (She's bad news).
> 'L' is for Loopy,
>   (Her fortunes stink).
> 'L' is for Loony,
>   (That's what we think).
> 'Y is for Yuccky,
>   (She's a fink).
> Put 'em all together,
> And what have you got?

Molly Harter,
Molly Harter,
Molly Harter,
Yuck!"

Just as they were finishing Mrs. Marnock came out onto the playground. She walked over to where I was standing. I guess I must have looked upset.

"What happened, Molly? Is something wrong?"

Janet and Lori came outside. Janet was carrying a jump rope. She waved at me and motioned for me to come over to where she and Lori were standing.

"I—I've got to go," I told Mrs. Marnock.

"Molly," she said, "are you sure you're all right?"

"I've got to go," I said, not answering her question.

How could I? The truth was that just then I was pretty sure I'd never be okay again for the rest of my life.

I didn't tell Janet and Lori what had happened. But they noticed something was wrong, because Lori asked me if I was coming down with a cold or something.

Later, at lunchtime, after they'd found out, they were both mad at me.

"Why didn't you tell us what happened?" Lori asked.

I just shrugged.

"You ought to have punched Norma in the nose," Lori said. "She's the one who starts everything."

I didn't say anything. I took my sandwich out of its plastic bag. It was corned beef. Not my favorite.

"Molly," Lori said softly, "everybody gets teased, especially by a bully like Norma." I knew she was trying to make me feel better.

"Not me," I said. "Not anymore. I'm not going to do anything ever again that Norma or Jackie or Clare or Carrie can tease me about."

Janet smiled. "It's going to get boring around here,"

69

she said. She unwrapped her sandwich. It was peanut butter.

"I—I'm serious, Janet. You're new around here and so you can't know what Norma's like. She's the kind of person who can make the other kids act crummy to you if she doesn't like you—the way she made Jackie and Clare and Carrie act crummy at recess. And she's worse if you do stuff she can make fun of. And I'm not going to ever again do anything she can make fun of. I—I'm making a promise to myself that I won't."

We ate our sandwiches and nobody said anything for a while. Then Janet asked if we were going to the city's anniversary party Saturday. I guess she was trying to find a new subject to talk about.

"I'm going," Lori said. "I'm dying to meet Loretta Lorne. Mom says she named me after her. Mom and Loretta Lorne went to Brampton Hills High together. And Mom says she's just the same now as she was in high school—always losing weight and gaining it back. Mom says Loretta Lorne always won two kinds of contests back in high school: beauty contests and pie-eating contests."

"My mom read an article about her in the Brampton Hills *Herald* last night," Janet said. "It said that she's at a diet farm right now, slimming down for her appearance at the mall."

"I read that too," Lori said. "Did you see the part about the big drawing the city's holding the morning of the party? The prize is a brand-new car. Brampton Motors donated it for the raffle. My mom's on the ticket committee. She says the tickets are selling like hotcakes."

Lori was sticking her hand into her lunch bag as she talked. Her hand was halfway out when she said, "Oh, yuck!"

"What's the matter?" Janet asked.

Lori pulled out her dessert. It was a Jolly Jelly bar.

Janet wrinkled her nose.

"Ugh!" she said. "My mom bought a pack of those too. She said the TV commercials made Jolly Jelly sound pretty good. But I wouldn't let her put one in my lunch."

"They are the worst," Lori said. She was looking at the Jolly Jelly with the same expression on her face Becka gets when we have spinach for dinner.

"Here," I said, pulling my usual dessert—a Chocky Chunka sample pack—out of my bag. "Let's share these."

I opened the pack and gave Janet and Lori each a cookie.

"Hey," Lori said when she took a bite, "this is *good*. Are these the cookies your mom makes?"

I nodded.

"They're great. Where do they sell these?"

I told her a few of the stores I knew about.

"My mom doesn't shop at any of those places," Lori said. "She shops at Farmer Fred's mostly. How come your mom doesn't get Farmer Fred's to sell her cookies?"

I gave Lori a look.

"Oh," Lori said. "You mean she's tried?"

I nodded.

"Mr. Glemp's just not interested. He told her he already has five different kinds of chocolate-chip cookies at his stores and that he doesn't want any more. In fact," I said, swallowing hard before I could finish my sentence, "I'm pretty sure that in a few more weeks my mom will be *out* of business."

"But these are *good*," Lori said. "Too bad my mom

71

had to see a big Jolly Jelly bar dancing across the TV screen instead of a Chocky Chunka cookie."

"Speaking of TV," Janet said, "did you hear Norma and Clare talking this morning, about the city's anniversary party, and how they're going to be on the five o'clock news because Clare's mother said that Channel 6 is going to send a cameraman to report on the party? Sounds like they think this is their big chance to get on TV."

"I'm glad I'm not *that* vain," I said, crunching up the empty Chocky Chunka wrapper and dropping it into my lunch bag. "So you get on the five o'clock news. So a few thousand people in Brampton Hills see you. So—"

I stopped.

"Molly," Janet said, "are you okay? You look a little funny."

For a minute I didn't say anything. I couldn't. It was as though all of a sudden all these different wheels had started turning in my head.

Finally I turned to my friends.

"Janet, Lori," I said, "I have an idea."

I told them all about my plan. Janet and Lori listened without saying anything. When I finished I said, "Well, what do you think?"

"I—I think it's a terrific idea," Janet said. "Except—"

"What?"

"Remember what you just told Lori and me? About not letting Norma see you doing anything that she could tease you about?"

"Maybe she won't find out," I said.

"I don't know, Molly," Janet said. "It's the kind of thing that's hard to keep a secret—especially if your plan works out the way you want it to."

I was quiet for a moment. I thought about everything

that might happen if I went ahead with my plan. I thought about what it would be like if Norma found out.

"I—I don't care," I said slowly. "I have to help my mom."

Chapter Eleven
Grandma Comes Through

As soon as Mrs. Marnock let us out of school I raced home, grabbed my bike, and pedaled as fast as I could up Morningside and down Forrester to Parker Avenue.

In less than fifteen minutes I was pressing the buzzer to my Grandma Mundy's apartment. She lived in Apartment 110 at the Parkmont Avenue Apartments.

Grandma came to the door and let me in. She was wearing a jogging suit and a headband.

"Molly!" she said, smiling her big smile and bending over to give me a hug. "I just finished exercising along with my videotape. I feel fantastic. Fit as a fiddle. Come on along, child. Come and sit at the table and I'll pour a nice health drink for both of us."

I went and sat at the table in Grandma's kitchenette.

"Grandma, there's something I want to talk to you about."

"Now, now, dear. First let's drink our Banana Wheat Germ Delights."

Grandma tilted her glass up and drank her Banana Wheat Germ Delight. When she put her glass down it was empty. She sat there, looking at me. She was waiting.

I held my breath, put the glass to my lips, and started to drink. Grandma smiled.

"There," she said happily. "Isn't that simply scrumptious?"

I nodded. I couldn't exactly tell her the truth—that the Banana Wheat Germ Delight tasted like wallpaper paste.

Somehow I finished the drink. Grandma tried to pour me a refill, but I put my hand over my glass and told her I didn't want to be greedy.

"Grandma," I said quickly, "do you remember, just before Halloween, you told me you'd be glad to make a costume for me?"

"Hmmm?" Grandma said. She'd gotten up from the table and gone to the refrigerator to get out a loaf of nut bread. She was busy slicing it.

"Oh, why, yes, of course I do, dear," Grandma said, placing a thick slice of nut bread down in front of me. "I enjoy making Halloween costumes for you girls. It reminds me of my days in the shop."

"And do you remember," I said, "how you told us to use our imaginations when we thought about what we wanted to be for Halloween because you could sew *any* kind of costume we wanted, no matter how hard it sounded to make?"

Grandma drew herself up and stuck out her chin. There was a proud look on her face.

"Never, in all my thirty years as a dressmaker," she said, "was there any project Ellen Mundy had to turn down."

Then Grandma looked kind of puzzled.

"But, sweetheart," she said, "Halloween's over. Why are we talking about Halloween costumes now, in the middle of November?"

I told Grandma my plan.

"Will you help me, Grandma?" I finally asked. "Will you?"

Grandma smiled.

"Of course I'll help, Molly," she said. "I think your idea's wonderful. It might really draw some attention to Hattie's business."

When I got home half an hour later Mom was on the phone.

"Well, how lovely," Mom said when she finally hung up.

"What's lovely?" I asked.

"John Digbert has asked me to go with him to the city's anniversary party at the mall. He's on the city board and he's been invited to sit with the guests of honor on the stage at the opening ceremonies. That means I'll be sitting there too."

"Oh," I said.

"Now, Molly," Mom said. "I know that you don't care for John Digbert too much. But do try and be fair, dear. Actually, when you get to know him, he's a caring, generous person."

"Generous! Mom, you know what everybody says about the Digberts. That they don't care about anything but money."

"Molly, I won't have you talk like that about John," Mom said sharply. "He's a very sweet person."

Sure, I thought.

I didn't care what Mom said. I knew better. Whatever Mr. Digbert was, he wasn't sweet. He was persistent though, that was for sure. Becka's dumping popcorn over him hadn't discouraged him from wanting to go out with Mom. I guess if you're Mr. Digbert little things like a greasy bowl of popcorn don't scare you away all that easily.

Friday night Grandma Munday called. She told me she'd finished the costume.

"It's pretty bulky," Grandma said. "I'll have to drive you to the mall in my van tomorrow."

"Okay, Grandma," I said. "I'll be there at ten."

I didn't sleep too well the night before the city's anniversary party. But when it was finally morning I wasn't tired at all, just kind of excited and a little bit scared.

I listened to the sounds of the house waking up—the front door opening when Mom got the Saturday paper from the porch, coffee perking, eggs cracking, bacon sizzling on the skillet, toast popping up out of the toaster, Nikki's and Becka's slippers padding on the staircase on the way downstairs, music from a Road Runner cartoon floating up the stairway from the rec room.

I got dressed and went downstairs.

Nikki was at the table in the kitchen, sipping orange juice.

"Where's Mom?" I asked.

"Doing her hair in the bathroom. She's getting ready for her date with Mr. D."

I told Nikki to tell Mom I was going to the party with Grandma.

"Aren't you going to have some breakfast?" Nikki asked.

I shook my head no and scooted out the back door to the garage. The bagful of Chocky Chunka samples and my tan tights and leotards from ballet class were where I'd put them last night, in my bike basket.

I pedaled as fast as I could to the Parkmont Apartments.

When I walked into Grandma's apartment, I saw the costume lying on her sofa.

"Grandma," I said, "it's great!"

Grandma beamed.

"Come on, Molly," she said. "I'll help you put it on."

About ten minutes later I was standing in front of the full-length mirror on Grandma's closet door, and staring me back in the face was the World's Largest Chocky Chunka Cookie. Me.

Grandma *was* a terrific seamstress. The costume was great. It was made out of tan fabric—that was the dough part—and brown fabric—the chocolate chips. Where my face was—a little bit above the middle of the cookie—Grandma had sewn in this brown screeny fabric that looked like one of the chocolate chips. That way I could see out, but no one could see me inside.

I was a five-foot-round chocolate-chip cookie with arms and legs. The tan tights and leotard sleeves made my legs and arms match the cookie fabric.

"Thanks, Grandma," I said, turning carefully so that I could give her a hug. "The costume's terrific."

"Oh, I enjoy sewing, Molly. It's fun for me. You know that." Grandma was quiet for a moment. Then, softly, she added, "I think your plan is a pretty good one, dear, and I hope it works out the way you'd like it to. But, Molly, if it doesn't I hope you won't be too disappointed. There are so many activities planned for the city's anniversary party that—well—people, uh, especially TV people, just may not pay much attention to a girl in a cookie costume."

"Grandma," I said, "I've got to do something. I don't want Mom to have to give up her cookie business. She loves it too much. And I don't want Mom to be worried all the time, the way she is now."

"Is it that bad, Molly?"

I folded my arms.

"It's the *worst*, Grandma. You know Mom. She's pretty, and smart, and terrific, and do you know who she's going out with today? Mr. *Digbert*. Mr. Digbert who's *awful* and *mean* and *crummy*. I bet if Mom weren't so upset and worried about her cookie business she wouldn't even think about dating Mr. Digbert."

Grandma smiled. It was a sort of a sad smile.

"Molly," she said, "I've known John Digbert since he was a toddler and—and I think you're 100 percent right. I think 'crummy' is exactly the word that describes him, and I've been tempted more than once to call Hattie and tell her she ought to have her head examined, going out with him."

"Why haven't you, Grandma?"

Grandma sighed.

"You're forgetting something, Molly. I've known your mother since she was *born*. And if I know anything about Hattie it's this: Once she's made up her mind to do something she'll do it, no matter what anyone says to her. If I criticized her seeing John Digbert, she'd only be more determined to see him.

"But I agree with you. Hattie has been upset lately, and certainly her worries about the cookie business might make John Digbert's company seem like a pleasant diversion."

All of a sudden Grandma took a second look at me, stepped back, and said, "Do you know, Molly, that this is the first time I've ever had a discussion this serious with a chocolate-chip cookie?"

I started laughing.

The next thing I knew the two of us were hugging each other. Or, at least, *I* was hugging Grandma. I knew she wanted to hug me back—but it isn't easy to hug anything that has a waist that's five feet across.

Chapter Twelve
The Big Day

Grandma drove me to the mall in her red van. I couldn't sit down in the cookie costume, so I rode standing in the back of the van. A blue car with the WWBH TV/Channel 6 logo on its doors was pulling to a stop just ahead of us when we finally arrived at the main entrance of the mall. The parking lot in front of the mall was full—crammed with cars and people.

I hadn't been to the mall for a long time. I wasn't crazy about shopping. What Bill the Clown had said was true: The mall had been roofed over. Before, the stores had been out in the open, with sidewalks in between them, but now everything was enclosed. I wasn't sure if I was going to like the changes. The only thing I'd really liked about visiting the mall was sitting on the outdoor benches waiting for Mom while she shopped and watching the birds fly through the sky overhead.

Well, I reminded myself, it didn't matter what I felt about the changes in the mall just then. I had a plan to work on, and the huge sign that was hanging over the main entrance to the mall reminded me of it.

**CITY OF BRAMPTON HILLS—
50TH ANNIVERSARY!
ELECTRIC LIGHT SHOW! BAND!
BALLOONS FOR THE KIDS!
SPEECH BY MAYOR COSGILL!
WIN A TURBODREAM SPORTS CAR!
GUEST OF HONOR: *MISS LORETTA LORNE*
CEREMONIES BEGIN 10 AM,
AT THE FOUNTAIN COURT**

The digital clock in Grandma's van read nine-fifty.

I got ready to step down out of the van. Then, just as I was about to slide the door open, I saw something that made me freeze.

Four girls were sauntering up the concrete walkway that led from Newly Avenue to the mall. It was Norma and her gang: Clare and Jackie and Carrie. My fingers tightened around the bag of Chocky Chunkas samples I was holding.

The funny thing was, I'd known Norma and her friends would be at the mall. I'd heard them talk about it. But until just then, as I was getting ready to step out of Grandma's van with the cookie samples I was planning to give out, I'd managed not to think about it too much.

Now my mouth had gone dry and my heart was pounding crazily and I was glad I hadn't eaten breakfast because my stomach felt queasy.

A bald man in a station wagon in back of us started beeping his car horn impatiently. I pulled the van doors open and carefully climbed down to the pavement. I looked back at Grandma and waved. Grandma returned my wave, then slowly drove away.

I was on my own.

I guess I expected that as soon as I stepped out of the van dressed in my cookie costume the swarms of people who were making their way to Fountain Court, the big court in the center of the mall, would pay all kinds of attention to me. And it was important for people to notice me, because if *they* noticed me the TV crew from WWBH TV would notice me too.

"Oh, look at the kid in the cookie costume," I expected people to say. And that would be my cue to walk over to them, hand them free sample packs of Mom's cookies, and tell them to ask their supermarket managers to stock Chocky Chunkas at their stores.

I would give out my sample packs. People would try Mom's cookies and love them. They would ask their food-store managers to stock Chocky Chunkas. And, best of all, the reporter from WWBH TV would notice the World's Largest Cookie walking around the Brampton Hills Mall and he would come over and interview me. And that would be my Big Chance: my chance to make a free TV commercial for Chocky Chunkas.

I knew exactly what I was going to say: "I am here representing Chocky Chunka cookies. Chocky Chunkas are made with 100 percent natural ingredients. If you want to try the most delicious chocolate-chip cookie in Michigan—and maybe even the world—try Chocky Chunkas."

The WWBH TV cameras would film my message and everyone who watched the WWBH TV news that evening would hear it. People would start demanding that their food stores carry Chocky Chunkas. Mom's cookie business would be saved.

Anyway, that was the plan. That was the way it was supposed to work out.

But that's not exactly the way it did work out.

The way it did work out was this:

Grandma's van rolled away, and there I was, dressed as the World's Largest Cookie, standing in the middle of the crowd that was working its way toward the mall and *hardly anybody even looked in my direction*.

Did you ever have a nightmare about going to school and then looking down and realizing you've come to school in your underwear? Well, the feeling I had that morning at the mall was kind of like that—except it was the opposite. I mean, I'd come to the mall dressed to get everyone's attention, and *nobody was looking at me at all*.

"It's her!" someone shouted. "It's Loretta Lorne."

"She's gorgeous!" another voice piped up.

"She's lost weight again," a woman's voice said admiringly.

"Yeah, for the fiftieth time," someone else said, loudly.

No wonder no one was paying any attention to me. There it was, just a few yards away from me—Loretta Lorne's limousine with Loretta Lorne getting out of it.

She was dressed, head to foot, in shimmery white: white gown, white mink, white slippers. Even her fluffy hair looked silvery white.

She looked like a Barbie doll come to life. And on her finger was the biggest diamond ring I had ever seen. It was as big as a Ping-Pong ball. It sparkled and glittered in the light from the flashbulbs that were popping off all around her.

Someone was waiting for her at the mall door. I recognized Mayor Cosgill. He came forward with a proud look on his face and escorted Loretta Lorne along a roped-off pathway. As soon as she disappeared into the mall, the crowd outside hurried in after her. When the crowd had thinned down enough so that I could pass through the mall doors without the wiring that shaped my costume getting all bent out of shape, I followed them in.

A few minutes later I got to Fountain Court. A stage had been set up for the day's ceremonies at the far end of the court. Around the stage a sort of a round arch had been built out of wood and you could see little glass bumps stuck all over the arch. I guessed that the little bumps were the electric lights for the electric-light show that would be part of the day's events.

The stage was pretty big, big enough to seat at least twenty people. Mom and Mr. Digbert were among the people sitting on the stage. And I recognized somebody else too: Fred Glemp. Fred Glemp, the owner of the Farmer Fred Supermarket chain, was sitting up on the stage along with the other special guests. I recognized him from his Farmer Fred TV commercials, even though for the anniversary party he was wearing a regular business suit instead of the Farmer Fred straw hat and overalls he wore on TV.

The biggest store in the Fountain Court area was just behind the stage. It was Dooley's. Dooley's was a children's clothing store where Mom used to buy a lot of my clothes when I was a toddler. When Nikki and I were younger we used to like to watch the robins build their nests in the O's of the Dooley's sign.

There weren't any robins now. Not with the new roof they'd built over the mall. Other things had changed too. Now there were open booths and stands in Fountain Court. A little to the left of the stage was a booth called Basketeeria. It sold wickerware and baskets. To the right

85

of the stage there was a stand that sold pop and hot pretzels.

I looked back up at the stage. I didn't see Loretta Lorne or Mayor Cosgill. I guessed that they had ducked into one of the mall offices and were probably waiting to make a big entrance.

Spotting Mom on the stage again made me feel guilty for a minute—I knew that, shy as Mom was about bragging up her own cookies, she probably would have been embarrassed if she knew what I was up to.

I began to wonder if my plan was such a great idea after all. But the way things were working out, it didn't look as though Mom would ever find out what I was up to anyway. I wondered if maybe Grandma had been right. With Loretta Lorne about to go onstage not too many of the people milling around Fountain Court that morning were very interested in looking at a kid in a cookie costume.

And if the crowd in the courtyard didn't pay any attention to me, the TV crew from Channel 6 wouldn't notice me at all.

Just then a microphone came to life with a sudden crackling sound. Somebody was clearing his throat. I looked over at the center of the stage. A man with a big red mouth and a huge red ball of a nose was grinning at the audience. It was Bill the Clown.

"Well, hello there, ladies and gentlemen *and* kiddies —heh, heh, heh. This is Bill the Clown welcoming you to a very important occasion—a party to celebrate the FIFTIETH ANNIVERSARY of the city of BRAMPTON HILLS!"

He waited for a cheer. The crowd gave a weak sort of cheer. I guess they didn't like Bill the Clown any more than I did. I only half-listened to what Bill the Clown was saying. I was too upset by the way my plan just wasn't working out to concentrate too much on what he was talking about. I was thinking about how, if things kept going the way they were, I'd have to telephone Grandma to pick me up a lot sooner than we'd planned.

"Wow," a voice close to me said. "I guess somebody doesn't know Halloween is over."

The voice was familiar. I wheeled around and faced her. Norma Digbert.

Chapter Thirteen
A Winner

Jackie and Carrie and Clare were standing behind her, grinning.

"Uh, do I know you?" Norma said.

I didn't answer her. Norma stood there staring at me for just about forever.

"C'mon," Clare finally said, "let's go."

Norma was turning around. She was just about to leave when she happened to look down. Her eyes narrowed.

I saw what she was looking at: my sneakers. Norma had seen my old, beat-up sneakers in gym class thousands of times.

I could tell that she was thinking hard. I could also tell that she couldn't quite remember why my sneakers looked so familiar.

I held my breath.

"Say," Norma said, pressing her face close to the screen that I was looking out of. "Who are you anyway?

I was about to say something, to answer her back. Then I remembered the day Norma and her friends had led the cheer against me on the playground, how awful I'd felt when they'd made fun of me. And I remembered how I'd promised myself I wouldn't ever again give them anything to tease me about.

I didn't answer Norma back.

Norma didn't give up though. Instead she stepped even closer to me. Her face, with its mean smile, was one inch away from mine. Only the chocolate-chip screen separated us.

I didn't know how anybody else would feel about having Norma Digbert's face one inch away from her own. But I wasn't too crazy about it. I took a step backward.

I didn't see the low edge of the planter stand behind me. My heel caught against it and I lost my balance. For a few seconds I teetered, my arms flailing, my bag of samples flying out of my hand.

Norma could have easily grabbed my arm, steadied me, and kept me from falling. But she didn't. I fell over backward into a clump of mums.

Norma, looking down at me, covered her mouth to hide her grin. What a crumb!

Clare looked embarrassed. Bending down, she helped me get up on my feet. She scooped up my bag of free samples and handed them back to me.

"What did you do that for?" Norma said, annoyed.

"I can help someone if I want to," Clare said. She sounded as annoyed as Norma.

Norma stared hard at Clare for a few seconds, then she blinked and turned around.

"Come on," she said, turning to leave, "let's go."

I watched the four of them stride off together. And I

stood there alone. Molly Harter, the world's largest chocolate-chip cookie. I felt like a dope.

Nothing was working out the way I'd planned it. Nothing. For a minute I just wanted to give up, find a phone, call Grandma to pick me up, and then forget I'd ever thought I could help save Mom's cookie business.

But I couldn't do that. I couldn't let Grandma down after all her hard work. Most of all I couldn't let Mom down—I had to try. I started to walk around. I gave sample packs of cookies to people who were standing around the courtyard.

And then it happened: People did begin to notice me. Maybe it was because Loretta Lorne was taking forever to make her big appearance and the crowd in the courtyard was starting to get bored. Or maybe I'd been wrong before, about people not being interested in a five-foot-round cookie. Maybe they just hadn't seen me when I was hanging back at the edge of the crowd.

Whatever the reason, some people did start to notice me. A few of them laughed and smiled and pointed. And the people who got the free samples I was handing out seemed really happy to get them.

A few people even opened the sample packs and took a bite of the cookies. Whenever they did they usually said things like "Good cookies," and, "Wonder where you can buy these?"

I told them to talk to their supermarket managers to ask them to stock Mom's cookies.

"Remember," I said, "these cookies are Chocky Chunkas! And they're the best chocolate-chip cookies in Michigan—and maybe even the world."

But even though I did start to get some attention, it wasn't much. Not enough, anyway, for the TV people from Channel 6 to notice me.

I looked over at the stage set up in front of Dooley's.

90

The WWBH TV news cameraman was standing at the top of the stairs, looking bored, his camera not aimed at anything.

I sighed. I started to feel really foolish. I must have been dreaming, thinking that anyone from the TV news would pay any attention to me, a kid in a cookie costume, when a world-famous movie star was visiting town.

But I kept on walking around and handing out the cookie samples—I didn't know what else to do. Finally I'd given them all out, except for one pack. I hadn't eaten breakfast *or* lunch and I was starting to get hungry. It was hard to eat in my costume, though, so I stuck the last pack into a little chocolate-chip pocket Grandma had sewn onto the front of my costume for my phone-call money.

I figured I could eat the cookies when I was back in Grandma's van.

I looked over at the stage again. Bill the Clown was still at the mike, laughing and joking with the crowd.

"Yes, sir, folks,' he was saying, "the raffle to benefit the city hospital has been MOST successful! We've raised ENOUGH MONEY to fully equip a NEW WARD!!! And, in a FEW MOMENTS we'll know which lucky Brampton Hills citizen is going to win the GRAND PRIZE: a shiny new Turbodream sports car. Yes, sir, in just a few short moments one of you lucky people will be the GRAND PRIZE WINNER of A BRAND NEW SPORTS CAR!!!

"Just think of it. Miss Loretta Lorne, one of our own hometown girls, will, in a few short moments, emerge from the mall office, walk up these stage steps, and pick from our drum the ticket which will name the WINNER of the BRAND NEW SPORTS CAR!!!

"Yes, folks, as part of our city's anniversary celebra-

91

tion someone will be given the keys to this fantastic NEW CAR!! And just think: IT COULD BE YOU!!!"

Bill the Clown started jabbing his finger at people in the crowd.

"That's RIGHT!" he said. "It could be you, or you, or—" He stopped and pointed straight at me. "Or even the great big humongous COOKIE over there. Heh-heh-heh."

I wanted to disappear. People were applauding and laughing at the same time.

Except for Norma. She was standing a little distance off, but I could see her pretty clearly. *She* wasn't applauding at all. She just looked over in my direction and wrinkled her nose.

"Molly!"

I wheeled around. I was hoping Norma hadn't heard whoever it was who had called me by my name.

"Wh—who is it?"

"It's me—Grandma. I hope you don't mind, Molly, but I decided to stay here at the mall with you. It took me forever, but I was finally able to find a parking space. What's the matter, dear? You sound a little upset."

"I—I—" It all spilled out. "Oh, Grandma," I whispered, "it just hasn't worked out the way I planned it. Not at all."

"How do you mean? You're here, aren't you? You gave out your samples, didn't you?"

I told her what had happened, how only a few people had paid any attention to me—not enough to stir up any interest from the WWBH TV crew.

"The cameraman from the Channel 6 news hasn't looked twice at me," I said. "I—I was wrong, Grandma. I'm not going to be on the evening news. I'm not going to be able to tell all the people in Brampton Hills about Mom's terrific cookies. I—"

I couldn't talk anymore. Behind my face-mask screen the tears were trickling out my eyes and down my cheeks.

Just then we heard a sort of buzz go through the crowd. Bill the Clown was saying, over and over, "AND HERE SHE IS, FOLKS. AND HERE SHE IS . . ."

I blinked back my tears and looked over to the roped-off area that lead from the mall office to the stage steps. The crowd hushed. Mayor Cosgill and Loretta Lorne appeared. Gasps filled the air.

Loretta Lorne smiled and waved to the crowd. Her diamond ring glittered like the star on top of a Christmas tree. The mayor, walking proudly, guided her through the roped-off aisle and up the stage steps.

"She's thinner than her pictures," I whispered to Grandma.

"Much thinner," Grandma said. "I guess those fat farms can work wonders."

Bill the Clown stepped aside and Mayor Cosgill took the microphone. The mayor spoke about what a great city Brampton Hills was to live in and raise a family, and how it wasn't fifty years old, but fifty years young, and how its greatest resource was its people—that kind of thing. The usual Mayor Cosgill speech.

Usually people started yawning halfway into the mayor's speeches. But everyone at the anniversary party was too excited about seeing Loretta Lorne to get bored with what the mayor was saying.

Finally, the mayor said the words everyone was waiting for: "Ladies and gentlemen, may I, ahem, present to you, Miss Loretta, ahem, Lorne."

A big roar went up from the crowd. Loretta Lorne

walked to the mike. She walked slowly, as though she were moving underwater. When she finally took the mike and spoke to the crowd her voice was whispery and dreamy—just the way she sounded in her movies. Her speech was on the short side. She thanked Mayor Cosgill for the invitation he had extended to her, on behalf of the town, to appear at the city's anniversary party. She said that appearing at the anniversary party was one small way she could repay Brampton Hills for the good start it had given her in life.

Then she told everyone about her new picture—*Moon Over Michigan*—a comedy-adventure which just happened to be set in her home state and which would be out around Christmastime. She said she hoped everyone would see it.

When she finished talking the crowd went crazy clapping and cheering. Then, when things calmed down, Mayor Cosgill took the microphone again. At the same time the drummer from the community college band, which was seated in front of the stage area, beat out a drumroll and Bill the Clown wheeled a big green drum up to where Loretta Lorne and the mayor were standing. As the mayor started to speak, Bill the Clown grabbed the handle on the drum and started turning it around and around.

"And now, ladies and gentlemen," Mayor Cosgill said, "our, ahem, lovely guest of honor, Miss, ahem, Loretta Lorne, will reach into this drum and pick out a winning ticket. In just a few moments some, ahem, lucky person will be the proud owner of a brand new Turbodream sports car!"

Mayor Cosgill held up something that was twinkly and silvery. "And here they are," he said, "the keys to the, ahem, grand prize sports car."

"To add to the excitement of this moment," the mayor continued, "the mall's own Handy Hand Hardware Store has donated and set up the exquisite electric-light display you will see shortly. Ladies and gentlemen, we are, ahem, in for a real treat. Wired into the scaffolding you see framing this, ahem, stage area are two thousand electric lights that have been coded by computer to flash and twinkle to the tune of the *1812 Overture*."

Mayor Cosgill grinned and handed the sports car keys to Loretta Lorne. Loretta Lorne smiled her dreamy smile. Then she slowly lifted the keys up for everyone to see. The drummer rolled another drumroll.

Smiling again, and using the hand that wasn't holding the sports car keys, she reached past the door of the drum. I guess Loretta Lorne did everything in super slow motion because it seemed like forever before she finished snaking her hand around and around in the drum and finally picked a ticket. A big slow grin spread over her face and she floated her hand out of the drum and wafted the white slip of paper over to Mayor Cosgill.

"And here it is, folks," Mayor Cosgill said excitedly, "the, ahem, ahem, winning ticket. The ticket which will, which will let someone in our fair city drive away today in the shiny new silver Turbodream sports car donated for the raffle by Brampton Motors."

I wasn't too excited. I knew Mom had bought some tickets to the raffle. And I knew Grandma had too. But somehow I also knew, even before the mayor announced the name on the ticket stub, that no one in our family would win the sports car. Some complete stranger would probably be the winner.

I was only half right. No one in our family won. But the big winner wasn't exactly a complete stranger either.

There was another drumroll. Then the mayor made his announcement.

"The, ahem, winner of the brand new Turbodream is *John Wendell Digbert.*"

Everything after that seemed to happen at once: the band started playing the *1812 Overture,* the scaffolding all around the stage began to glitter and sparkle with the two thousand electric lights flashing on and off, and Mr. Digbert jumped up from where he was sitting next to Mom on the stage as if someone had given him an electric shock.

He wasn't exactly cool about his good luck. He lunged at Loretta Lorne, grabbed for the keys to the Turbodream he'd won, all the time yelling, at the top of his lungs, "Mine, mine—it's mine!"

People talked about what happened next and whose fault it really was for months after the anniversary party. Later on almost everyone agreed that Loretta Lorne panicked, that was all.

Not that anyone blamed Loretta Lorne. Sure, the Mr. Digbert most people knew was creepy, but he usually acted like a calm and quiet and ordinary person. However, the Mr. Digbert who was grabbing for his Turbodream sports-car keys the day of the city's anniversary party didn't act calm or quiet or ordinary at all.

So Loretta Lorne reacted pretty much the way any person who didn't have nerves of steel and who thought she was being attacked by a madman would react. Most people thought that it wasn't her fault that she panicked.

Sure, they agreed, she probably *should* have had her ring resized, after she'd finished slimming down on her latest big diet. But, as everyone also said, how was she to know that Mr. Digbert would lunge at her and frighten her the way he did when he grabbed for the keys? And that she'd scream and throw up her hands. And that because it would all happen at the exact same time that two thousand electric lights were flashing on and off it would be impossible to see where the half-million-dollar ring that flew off her hand landed.

Chapter Fourteen
The Big Search

The next thing anyone knew, Loretta Lorne was filling the air with an ear-piercing shriek.

"My ring!" she wailed. "My ring! Oh, it must have flown off when that—that madman lunged at me. Oh, my ring. My beautiful, priceless diamond!"

The band stopped playing. The flashing electric lights stopped flashing. None of the city council members or their guests on the stage looked too cheerful anymore. Except for Bill the Clown. But his smile was painted on.

"Uh, ladies and gentlemen," Mayor Cosgill said soberly, "it appears that we've, ahem, had a misfortune. It appears that our lovely guest of honor has—has lost a ring which is of great, ahem, sentimental value to her."

"It's worth half a million dollars!" Loretta Lorne wailed.

At that point several of the city council members got off their chairs and onto their hands and knees to search for the missing ring.

"If anyone, *anyone*, has, ahem, seen where our lovely guest's ring landed—please let us know."

Just then Fred Glemp, who'd been watching everything that had been happening with a concerned look on his face, stood up, walked over to Mayor Cosgill, and tapped him on the shoulder. The two men bent their heads together and whispered to one another. Mayor Cosgill nodded and then took the microphone again.

"Mr. Fred Glemp, owner of the Farmer Fred supermarkets, has, ahem, generously stepped forth to offer an appropriate reward—in the amount of *one hundred dollars*—to whoever locates the missing article."

A buzz went through the crowd. People who were close to the front of the stage started to get down on their hands and knees and scrabble around.

Loretta Lorne whispered something in the mayor's ear. Mayor Cosgill took the microphone again.

"Perhaps," he suggested, "the, ahem, missing article landed further back."

That was all he needed to say. Soon almost everybody in the mall courtyard was scurrying around and searching for the missing ring.

I wished I could join them. A hundred dollars would help Mom to pay off some of her cookie business bills. But dressed in the cookie costume I couldn't even bend over.

"I don't believe it," I heard Grandma say. "I just don't believe it."

"Believe what?" I asked her.

"Look at that greedy child over there," Grandma said.

I looked over to where Grandma was pointing and then I knew what she meant. It *was* pretty unbelievable.

It was Norma Digbert. Norma wasn't just scurrying around, like everyone else. She was knocking people over, left and right, pushing them out of her way so that she could look for the missing ring. Her face looked wild and frantic, sort of the way I imagined a hungry shark would look when he was searching for his next meal.

I guess I wasn't the only one who thought Norma was acting freaky. Carrie and Jackie and Clare weren't even looking for the ring themselves. They were just looking at Norma, staring at her with their eyes popped open.

"Out of my way," Norma was yelling, pushing at whoever happened to be in her path. "Get out of my way. I want that reward money. I want to win that money. I have to have it. One hundred dollars. One hundred—"

"Well," Grandma said, "that is one greedy child."

"I guess it runs in the family," I explained to Grandma. "That's Norma, Mr. Digbert's niece."

Speaking about Mr. Digbert made me remember him. I glanced up to the stage area. Mr. Digbert was still standing by the microphone, holding the keys to his Turbodream in front of his face and beaming. I don't think he cared too much about Loretta Lorne's ring or anything else. I wondered what Mom was thinking. I looked over to where she was sitting but her face didn't have any expression at all. She was just looking in front of her.

A minute ticked by.

And then two.

And then three.

And then, finally, ten.

And nobody found the ring!

Not even Norma. And she was trying harder than anybody else, knocking old ladies and toddlers out of her way as she scoured the tiled floor of the courtyard.

By the time ten minutes had passed, the police had arrived. Loretta Lorne, in tears, was explaining to one of the policemen, whom I recognized as Officer Brenner, how her ring had flown off her hand when Mr. Digbert had come to grab the keys to the car he'd won. Because they were standing so near the microphone, everybody in the courtyard could hear what she was saying.

"It was the diet," Miss Lorne wailed. "I just finished a diet. I've lost twenty pounds. That's a lot for a person who's only five-feet-two. I—I didn't have time to get my ring resized before coming here and now—now it's missing. I—I should have stayed fat."

Everybody felt pretty bad for Loretta Lorne. After all, she was a guest in our town. If I'd been the person who'd grabbed the keys from her hand and made her lose her ring I know I would have been pretty embarrassed. But not Mr. Digbert.

Mr. Digbert was busy clipping the keys to his Turbodream into his key holder as Miss Lorne spoke to Officer Brenner. He had a grin on his face that probably wouldn't come off unless someone told him there'd been a mistake and he wasn't the prizewinner after all. He didn't care that he'd made Loretta Lorne lose her fabulous ring. All he cared about was that he'd won the car.

"It's all—it's all that *madman's* fault!" Miss Lorne said, pointing a shaking, angry finger at Mr. Digbert. "He—he startled me, and my hands flew up, and now," she wailed, "my beautiful ring is lost, gone, and no one's been able to find it!"

For the first time, Mr. Digbert seemed to notice what was going on around him. He cleared his throat and drew himself up stuffily.

"It is not *my* fault, madam," Mr. Digbert said, "that *you* lost your composure." He turned to Mayor Cosgill and Mr. Glemp. "Why this overexcitable woman was chosen to present the grand prize, I'll never know."

Loretta Lorne gasped and said, "Oh," in a small,

strangled voice, and started sniffling. Officer Brenner and Mayor Cosgill and Bill the Clown glared at Mr. Digbert. At least I thought Bill the Clown did too—it was hard to tell because of the makeup.

"Now, look here, Digbert," Mayor Cosgill was saying.

He never got to finish though, because all of a sudden, a loud, shrill scream filled the air.

"What was that?" Janet asked. She'd gotten to the mall late but had managed to find me and Grandma in the crowd.

We turned in the direction of the scream—just in time to see Norma diving headfirst into the Fountain Court fountain. For a few seconds she was thrashing about wildly, throwing up sprays of water and splattering everyone around her as she worked her way to a spot in the middle of the fountain. For a second she disappeared under the water, then she bobbed back up, waving her hand wildly over her head and screaming.

"I've got it," she was screaming. "I've found the ring! I saw it shining in the middle of the fountain where nobody else was smart enough to see it. I've got it! I have it! I win! I win the reward! Me! Norma Digbert! *I* win it! I do! Me! I win!"

"That girl is *bonkers*," Grandma whispered.

Grandma probably wasn't the only one who thought so. The crowd in the courtyard was hushed. Everyone was staring at the screaming, dripping wet girl in the middle of the fountain whose long blond hair, thick with water, hung down the front of her face like a mask.

And then everybody reacted at the same time: Loretta Lorne stopped sniffling, Officer Brenner hurried off the stage and down to the edge of the fountain where he leaned over to help Norma out, and I had my flash.

That was just what it was like: like a flashbulb popping off in my mind.

"Oh, no!" I said, gasping.

"What's wrong?" Grandma asked.

"It's—I—Grandma," I whispered, "Norma doesn't have the ring. She can't have it."

"She can't? But, Molly, you saw her—she found it. In the fountain."

"But that's not where it landed."

"But, Molly, she's got it in her hand."

"She's wrong. She doesn't. Look."

I pointed to where Officer Brenner was helping Norma climb out of the water.

"Here it is!" Norma shouted. "I spotted it. It was glittering in the water. I saw it. Me. I win the award. I found it. I found the ring."

Loretta Lorne, not moving slowly now, was running down the pavilion steps toward Norma and Officer Brenner.

"Well?" Grandma said. She said it as though her point was made.

"I don't care," I said. "Whatever she found in the fountain, it's not the missing ring."

"*Molly,*" Grandma said, "I know you don't like the Digberts. I'm not exactly crazy about them myself at the moment. But it does look like your friend did—"

"*This is not my ring.*"

We both looked over to where Loretta Lorne was standing and peering into Norma's dripping wet hand. "This isn't a ring at all," Loretta Lorne shouted, "It's—it's a marble."

"Huh!" Norma yelled. "A marble?" She was clearing the hair out of her eyes frantically. "No. You—you're wrong. You—you have to be. It's—it's—" and then she stopped as she finally managed to clear the dripping

103

wet hair away from her face. She stared at the shiny glass object Loretta Lorne was frowning at, and broke into a long wail.

"Aaaaagh! It *is* a marble. I was wrong. I thought I saw the ring. I thought I had it. I thought I found it. And it was only a dumb marble. And—and I'm all wet and drippy! And—and these are my brand-new stirrup pants —and—aaaagh!"

"Your, uh, friend Norma's freaking out," Grandma whispered.

Nobody paid any attention to Norma. No one at all. Loretta Lorne started sniffling again. Officer Brenner was patting her on the shoulder. Mayor Cosgill was talking in a low voice to several of the councilmen on the stage. And the people gathered in the courtyard were back on their hands and knees searching every inch of Fountain Court for the ring that was still missing.

"Molly," Grandma said, as if she were just realizing something, "you were right. Norma didn't find the ring! But—but how did you know? Ahead of time like that?"

Grandma had her fingers on my arm. She was pressing it, hard.

"You saw where it landed!" she whispered excitedly. "That's it, right, Molly?"

I shook my head no. Then I realized Grandma couldn't see my head shaking inside the cookie costume, so I said, "Uh-unh—I didn't exactly *see* where it landed. But I just *knew* Norma was wrong."

Grandma looked puzzled.

"You didn't exactly see? But you knew? But how, Molly?"

"I—I just did, Grandma. I—I had this flash—just like the flash I had when Becka was lost in the sewer."

"ESP," Janet whispered excitedly. "It's your ESP again. Molly, you know where the ring is, don't you?"

"Molly, if you know where the ring is, you have to do something." Grandma looked really happy. I knew what she was thinking. Here was my chance to get on TV in my Chocky Chunka costume.

"But if I'm wrong..." I stopped in midsentence. I wasn't afraid of being wrong. I'd promised myself I wouldn't do anything that Norma could tease me for. Now I had to do something she'd probably kill me for. I, Molly Harter, had to get up onstage in a chocolate-chip cookie costume and show up Norma Digbert.

I tried not to think about Norma. I tried to think about the dancing Jolly Jelly bar on the *Bill the Clown Show*. I tried to think about Mom and how hard she was working to make Chocky Chunkas a success. I took a deep breath.

"Grandma," I said, "wait right here."

"Molly, where are you going?" Grandma asked.

I didn't turn around to answer. I couldn't. It was hard work getting through the crowd to the stage dressed as a humongous cookie.

Chapter Fifteen
ESP Again

"Mayor Cosgill," I yelled as I ran up the wooden stairway to the stage, "Miss Lorne, Officer Brenner, I know where the ring is. I know where it is."

Up on the stage I turned around and looked out at the crowd. Everybody had stopped searching for the ring. Everyone was looking at me.

Then I turned the other way and looked over to where Mom was sitting. Mom was staring at me with a puzzled frown. I knew she didn't recognize me, but that she would pretty soon. Her expression was the same as it was when we used to go hiking and she'd try to guess the name of a songbird we'd hear.

I was glad Mom didn't recognize me just then. If she did I was pretty sure I'd be too nervous to tell Mayor Cosgill what I knew.

"Yes, young lady?" the mayor said excitedly. "You say you saw where the ring landed?"

"I didn't see where it landed," I blurted out. "I just know where it is. I—I have ESP."

Mayor Cosgill looked startled for a moment. Then he smiled in a tired way.

"Uh, yes," he said, reaching out to pat my hand with one of his own. "I've often met giant cookies who, uh, have ESP. Look, young lady, or whoever you are in that costume, I, ahem, appreciate your trying to lighten the tension of this moment with your little joke but—"

"I'm not joking, Mayor Cosgill. I do have ESP."

I looked out at the crowd. I looked over to where I knew Norma and Carrie and Jackie and Clare had been standing.

Norma was still standing next to the fountain, dripping wet. But Carrie and Jackie and Clare weren't with her. They were huddled in another section of the courtyard.

Norma had her hands on her hips and she was glaring at me. I didn't need ESP to know two things: one, that Norma had guessed it was me in the cookie costume; and, two, that she was angry. Angrier than I'd ever seen her.

The next thing I knew Norma was running toward me and screaming.

"I know who that cookie is," she was yelling. "It's Molly Harter, and she can't know where that ring is. She doesn't have ESP. She's a weirdo and a fake."

Quicker than you'd think someone in soggy wet clothes could run, Norma zipped up the stairs to where I was standing on the stage, and before I even realized what was happening, her quick hands snaked up and ripped at the costume I was wearing.

I heard fabric tear and fall away. Two seconds later, there I was, standing in front of the whole town of

Brampton Hills dressed in nothing but my tan tights and leotard, with shreds of costume fabric hanging around the wiring Grandma had used to give the costume its round shape.

"Molly!"

That was Mom's voice. I turned around. My cheeks felt pink and hot. Mayor Cosgill gave Norma and me a stern, disapproving look, and then he said, "Hattie Harter! I should have thought any daughter of yours would know better than to, ahem, prance around when the town is having a moment of crisis, and claim to have answers to problems that she can't possibly have answers to.

"And you," he said, wheeling to face Mr. Digbert, who was probably still thinking only about his big win, because he was still grinning from ear to ear. "And you," Mayor Cosgill repeated, "fine niece you have, Digbert—she goes around ripping costumes off her friends without a second thought."

"Molly does not lie."

That was Mom. She'd jumped up and come to stand next to me—or at least as close to me as she could get with the wires from my ruined costume in the way.

Then I heard Mr. Digbert speak up.

"Norma has done nothing wrong," he said. "It's simply that we Digberts do not allow hoaxes to be perpetrated on the public."

Mom gasped.

"John Digbert," she said coldly, "are you calling my daughter a liar?"

"Well," Mr. Digbert said coolly, "as they say in my business, 'If the shroud fits . . . wear it.' If anything at all is clear to me, Hattie, it's that your affection for your daughter is blinding you to the fact that she has some rather obvious, uh, faults."

108

"Oh!" Mom said. But it wasn't a hurt "Oh!" It was an angry one. "John Digbert," she said slowly, "the only obvious faults around here are—are the ones in your head!"

A roar of laughter rose from the crowd. It was only then that Mom and Mr. Digbert realized that their whole conversation was being picked up by microphone and broadcast to the crowd in the courtyard.

When the laughter settled down a voice near the front of the crowd yelled out, "Hey, so what's going on? Does this kid know where the ring is, or what?"

"Yes, Henry," another voice that was soft and whispery and came from just behind me said, "just what *is* going on here? Is is possible that—does this child know where my ring is? Perhaps we should let her—"

"I *do* know," I broke in excitedly. "I *do*. I had this flash. And I saw it. The ring, I mean. It's—it's in one of the Basketeeria baskets."

An excited murmur rose from the crowd. A few large men started to walk toward the Basketeeria stand.

Shreeeeee.

That was Officer Brenner's whistle.

"Hold it!" Officer Brenner said. "This is a police matter—locating a lost article. No one comes near the Basketeeria until it's been thoroughly searched."

A disappointed murmur spread through the crowd. But the men fell back.

Mom helped me to get out of what was left of my cookie costume. Then I followed Officer Brenner down the stage steps and over to the Basketeeria. The lady in charge, her face excited and her eyes wide, stepped aside and let me and Officer Brenner into the booth.

There were about two hundred baskets stacked on the shelves in the Basketeeria booth—large ones, small ones, round ones, square ones.

"Well," Officer Brenner said, "go ahead, young lady. Search through them and see if you can find the missing item."

Something was wrong. Something felt wrong. In my flash I'd seen Loretta Lorne's ring resting in a round, bowl-shaped container that was made out of straw. Now, the Basketeeria baskets were made out of straw, yes, and a lot of them were round, true, and they were shaped like bowls, of course, but . . .

"Officer Brenner," I began, "the ring isn't—"

"Go ahead, Molly," Officer Brenner said. His voice was kind. "Don't feel nervous now. If it helps you any, you should know that I haven't forgotten how you found your sister last month. That was ESP too, wasn't it?"

I nodded, feeling miserable. Something was all wrong.

"She doesn't know where the ring is."

A shrill voice that came from just behind me yelled in my ear. I wheeled around. It was Norma. She was still soggy wet and the face in the middle of all that wet stringy hair looked mean and spiteful.

I turned back around, determined to ignore her. I guess Norma didn't like that too well. I felt her hand sink into my shoulder like a steel claw. She was trying to twist it so that I had to turn around again and look at her. I tried to ignore her, but I couldn't. I couldn't shrug her hand off. My shoulder started to hurt.

I turned back around to face her. Her hand fell away. Norma was grinning her mean grin.

"Admit it, Molly Harter," she said. "You're lying. You don't know where the ring is. Your ESP is a fake."

I stared at Norma. I stared at her hard. And then, all of a sudden, tears started popping out of my eyes. Norma sounded jubilant.

"Ah-hah!" she crowed. "She's blubbering. The big

110

liar is blubbering because now everyone knows she's a *fake*."

But Norma was wrong. The tears that were spilling out of my eyes were the terrific kind of tears you cry when something wonderful has just happened to you.

"Officer Brenner," I yelled, "I know where the ring is now. I know where it it!"

I was looking past Norma, just above her head, at the big red plastic letters of the Dooley's sign that hung just behind the stage area.

"Now, Molly," Officer Brenner said.

"Officer Brenner," I said. "I *know*. Straw. A bowl shape. What I saw in my flash was the robin's nest up in the loop of the first O in the Dooley's sign. *That's* where the ring landed."

Chapter Sixteen
The Last Cookie

Fifteen minutes later—that's how long it took for the fire department to arrive with their ladders—a tall thin fireman began to climb up to the abandoned nest in the first O of the Dooley's sign.

Nobody said a word. All of the hundreds of pairs of eyes at the city's anniversary celebration were looking in the same direction. The Channel 6 cameraman was recording the action.

I couldn't breathe.

I stood next to Officer Brenner, shivering in my tights and leotard. Officer Brenner said he could get me a blanket if I wanted one.

"I'm not cold," I said.

That was true. All the parts of me that could feel anything were warm and tingly. I wasn't shivering from the cold.

The fireman was halfway up the ladder.

"Look, Molly," Officer Brenner whispered softly, "if

the ring isn't there, you don't have to feel bad. Everyone knows you were just trying to help."

As soft as Officer Brenner's voice was, I guess it wasn't soft enough. Norma heard him.

"Oh, sure," Norma said sarcastically. "The *weirdo* was just trying to *help*."

I looked over at Norma. It was funny. It was like I was seeing her for the first time: She stood there, soggy from head to foot because she'd thrown herself into the mall fountain to go after a marble. And she was calling *me* a weirdo.

I looked straight into Norma's eyes.

"Norma," I said, "I wouldn't call somebody else a weirdo if I went around swimming in two feet of water looking for a marble."

Carrie and Jackie started giggling. They were standing together close to where I was waiting with Officer Brenner. Clare was standing next to me too. So was Janet.

Norma was standing a little distance off. All by herself. She was still terrifically angry. But I didn't care too much anymore. I knew I'd never care too much ever again.

Up on top of the ladder something was flashing in the fireman's hand.

"It's *here*," he yelled down at the crowd. "Just like the kid said! How *about* that, huh?"

The next thing I knew Loretta Lorne was running over to me. A second later she was hugging me hard against her white mink coat.

"Oh, you dear thing," she said. "Now you and your parents must have dinner with the mayor and me tonight."

It took a few minutes but I explained to her about Mom's and Dad's divorce. She said that was all right. Mom and I would be her guests then.

113

"And, of course," she added, "if you have a best friend that you'd like to invite . . ."

A best friend? I had had a best friend. And then I'd lost her. Clare had been Norma's best friend since school began. And I remembered how I'd been almost sure, after what had happened in the first couple of months of school, that nobody ever again would be my best friend.

And now I knew that wasn't true.

"A best friend?" I said. "I—I think I do have one." And I looked past the suddenly friendly faces of Clare and Jackie and Carrie to where Janet was standing.

Janet smiled a big happy smile.

Loretta Lorne was smiling too. She slipped her ring back on her finger and then held it up to the light, twisting it this way and that so that it caught the light and glittered like a gigantic star. The cameraman from the Channel 6 news was still rolling his film. His camera was aimed at Loretta Lorne and the mayor and me.

"Oh!" she said. "I feel *so* happy! I wish I had something to celebrate this occasion with."

"Uh, champagne perhaps?" Mayor Cosgill suggested. "It would, ahem, be no problem to send for some."

"No. No. Not champagne," Loretta Lorne said. "I don't drink. Not at all. When I celebrate I celebrate with *food!* With something really yummy, something terrifically delicious—like, oh, a jelly-filled doughnut, or a piece of peach pie, or—or something like that. I don't know about you, Henry, but when I'm happy I like to EAT!"

And that was when it happened: another flash. Except it wasn't ESP this time. It was an *idea* flash.

"Uh, Miss Lorne," I said, *"wait right here. Don't move."*

"What?"

Loretta Lorne was blinking at me in a surprised way.

114

But I didn't stick around to explain. Instead I rushed over to the stage and dashed up the stairs. I found what I was looking for right away: the shreds of fabric that were left from my ruined chocolate-chip cookie costume. Rummaging around in the pile of cloth I found it: the pocket with the Chocky Chunka sample pack I'd put away for myself.

I dashed back with the sample pack in my hands to where Loretta Lorne was standing and chatting with Officer Brenner and Mayor Cosgill and Fred Glemp. The cameraman from Channel 6 still had his camera aimed at Loretta Lorne.

"Miss Lorne," I said, handing her the pack of Chocky Chunkas, "try these."

"Cookies!" Loretta Lorne said. "Chocolate-chip! Oh, I just *love* chocolate-chip cookies."

"Then you're *really* going to love these," I said, turning to face the lens of the camera the Channel 6 cameraman was aiming our way. Loudly I said, "These are Chocky Chunkas and they're the *best* chocolate-chip cookies in Michigan, or maybe even the world."

Loretta Lorne opened the pack of cookies. She picked one up and took a bite. Slowly she chewed the cookie. Then she swallowed. At first the only expression on her face was a sort of puzzled look.

Then it happened. Slowly, very slowly, a great big happy grin spread over Loretta Lorne's face.

"Why—why these are the *best* chocolate-chip cookies I've ever had!" she said. "Mmmm. They're *delicious!*"

She finished a cookie. Then she gobbled down another one. And one more. There was only one left. She was about to reach for that one when a funny thing happened: Before she could grab the last Chocky Chunka and pop it into her mouth, Fred Glemp, who had been standing behind Mayor Cosgill and watching everything

115

that had been going on, did something that was very impolite. He reached over, picked up the last cookie, looked at it, and then quickly popped it into his own mouth.

Loretta Lorne glared at him.

"Mmmmm," Fred Glemp said.

Then he turned to Miss Lorne with an apologetic look on his face. "I'm sorry, Miss Lorne," he mumbled. He finished chewing and swallowed the cookie. "But," he continued, "I own a chain of supermarkets and, well, I couldn't help notice your reaction to those chocolate-chip cookies you ate just now. I don't think I've ever seen anyone enjoy cookies that much before. And I— well, I'm sorry for being impolite, but Farmer Fred's *has* to keep up with the latest and the best in food products. I had to see what those marvelous cookies tasted like. Molly," he said, turning to me, "what did you say they were called?"

"CHOCKY CHUNKAS!" I yelled. "My mom makes them, and she's sitting right over there."

The next thing I knew Mr. Glemp was walking over to Mom with a big grin on his face.

"Hattie Harter," he said, "why didn't you tell me you made the best cookies in town?"

I have to give Mom credit. She kept her cool. She didn't remind Mr. Glemp that that was exactly what she'd tried to tell him only a couple of weeks ago, and that he just hadn't listened, and that he hadn't even wanted to *try* her cookies.

Instead she gave him a big smile. Then she thanked him for his compliment, winked at me, and pulled an order pad out of her purse.